UnSettled

UnSettled
and other stories

Sandra Hill

Published in 2015 by Modjaji Books
PO Box 385, Athlone, 7760, Cape Town, South Africa
www.modjajibooks.co.za
© Sandra Hill
Sandra Hill has asserted her right to be identified as
the author of this work.

Edited by Emily Buchanan
Cover artwork by Megan Ross
Cover text by Megan Ross
Book layout by Andy Thesen
Set in Bembo

Printed and bound by Megadigital, Cape Town
ISBN: 978-1-928215-14-1
ebook: 978-1-928215-15-8

for my
Mom and Dad

Acknowledgements

I am particularly grateful to Christine, Delia, Merle, Karin, Johann, Sally-Ann, Margie and Maire, who read and commented on my stories and to Sebastian and Phoebe who first suggested writing them. Your enthusiasm and support kept me buoyant. A special thanks to my editor Emily, who worked with warm-hearted rigour and generosity. And to Modjaji for making it rain.

Heartfelt thanks to Anne who taught me the most valuable lessons about writing.

Thanks to Antjie Krog for permission to quote from Krog, A. *Body Bereft*. Cape Town: Umuzi, 2006.

Five of these stories were written in partial fulfilment of a MA in Creative Writing at UWC, and have benefited from feedback from my two classmates, Jerome and Jolyn, and supervisor, Meg.

By Any Other Name was first published in 2013 by Umuzi in an e-book collection of short stories called *The Ghost Eater and Other Stories*.

A note on sources

While some of the people who appear in this collection of short stories actually lived, they appear in this book as fictional characters.

I am indebted to my aunt Dorothy for our family history *Four Families* (unpublished). Full of well researched information, interesting anecdotes, quotes and fabulous turns of phrase, it was a wonderful resource for the writing of 'South Bound'.

I am similarly indebted to my cousin Ian for his booklet *Isabella* (unpublished) which piqued my interest in our maternal great-grandmother resulting in the story 'Thicker than Water'.

Contents

South Bound

Eleanor is asleep under a jacaranda tree in her daughter's lush Escombe garden. Escombe is no longer part of the Natal Colony, the Natal Colony exists only in the minds of people like Eleanor. Escombe, though still in the same place it's always been, is now part of the Union of South Africa. It is the 20th of January 1923. Eleanor has lived in the Natal Colony for thirty years exactly. She has been married for only one day less.

Gladys's garden is wonderful, but according to Eleanor, not as wonderful as it could be with a little more effort. Gladys's bougainvillea are a riot of cerise, peach and white. Her dipladenias climbing the pillars of the front veranda – a profusion of pink. The creamy day lilies are in full bloom. The lavender is a field of purple and the plumbago hedge, where dragon-like chameleons lurk, is thick with blue ... a cool blue cloud at the bottom of the garden, Gladys thinks. Philemon is hard pressed to keep the monkeys from the guava, mango, paw-paw and avocado trees. Eleanor pays little heed to the real reason Gladys has no time for her lawns, beds, shrubs, hedges and trees. In a quarter of an hour or so, Gladys will lift Eleanor in her stout arms and carry her away from the heat into the cool of the house. It is not the time of year to be outdoors, but Eleanor insists on being in the garden.

'That's the way it's always been,' Gladys confides to her new husband, 'Mother insists and Gladys obeys.'

Eleanor is asleep under a jacaranda tree in her daughter's lush Escombe garden. The barometer has dropped. Eleanor does not notice the thickening of the air, nor how clammy her forehead. Her chair is covered with blankets and a white sheep fleece. It is the day-bed of a woman whose own padding has melted away, whose bones are dissolving, whose joints have swollen over.

'It won't be long,' whispers Walter to his bride as they lie side by side sweltering in the room next to Eleanor's, the door ajar so Gladys can hear her if she calls out. 'I'm afraid, it won't be for very much longer, my dear.'

Eleanor's book is lying on the grass. It is a very slim volume, the slimmest she owns and the latest addition to her collection, thanks to dear Cora who tracked it down somewhere in London and sent it over. Eleanor cannot hold anything heavier than the slimmest of books, nor can she make the pages turn one by one.

She reads Virginia Woolf's collection of short stories, *Monday or Tuesday*, published by Hogarth Press just two years earlier, in the most random of fashions. A page here, a paragraph there. What does it matter? Would the authoress object? Would she feel slighted if she knew an old (only fifty six mind you) ... would she mind if a woman riddled with arthritis was reading her latest book in so random a fashion that each character seeped into the next? Lily, the woman he might have married, the sad woman in the train, the sleeping Miranda, Castalia, Miss Thingummy. Would she mind that each story was losing its borders?

Eleanor had wanted to read the story 'Kew Gardens', and Gladys had opened the book to the right page, and placed it firmly in her hands. Eleanor reads the description of colours, patterns and plants before her eyes snag on the assertion that one always thinks of the past while lying under a tree in a garden.

Yes, she thinks, yes. That's it. That is what a garden does ... it makes you think of the past, of where you have come from.

Eleanor, thick-fingered, tries to turn the page. Oh bother, now the story is taking place on a train. Try again, Eleanor. Now at a tea party. Try again, fingers. Is this the right page? Is it still 'Kew Gardens', or a different story? Hard to tell. Now there are lovers on the grass, lying under a tree perhaps? He wants to take her hand, but oh, she's offering him her heart!

No, no don't! Never entrust your heart to a man, you foolish girl, idiot woman.

Eleanor, defeated, drops her book on the grass and drifts into a fretful sleep. She groans out loud: foolish girl, idiot woman. The birds, little black-headed orioles, pecking the paw-paw skins the maid arranged on the bird table where Eleanor could see them, hear the groan and fly off. The green mamba napping in the thick foliage of the orange clivias hears it and lifts his head. The monkeys in the mango tree hear it, stop chattering for a moment, and look about, thinking Philemon might be coming. Gladys, her hands mixing a batch of scones for tea, the butter already too soft to turn sifted flour into crumbs, hears it and pauses. Was that Mother calling? Would Daddy have heard? She'd turn the radio down but her hands are sticky with dough, besides it's her favourite programme and in a few minutes, the news. Walter likes her to listen to the news ... it makes dinner more interesting. Besides, Mother had insisted she wasn't to be disturbed till tea time. Gladys goes back to her mixing, back to her programme, hums along with the music. She'll check on the old girl as soon as the scones are in the oven. Pretty warm out there under the jacaranda tree.

Eleanor is asleep under the jacaranda tree in her daughter's lush Escombe garden dreaming about the past. And while she sleeps, she groans a long drawn out groan, as if puzzled, as if vexed. Perhaps she is wondering how it can be that women are still foolish enough to entrust their hearts to men? Perhaps she is thinking of her own choices? Life hasn't turned out the way she'd imagined. What was it that made her leave anyway? Has she ever regretted boarding that south bound ship? And why did she marry that man?

★

Cora's theory

It was an act of rebellion. That is what it was. And my sister Eleanor paid the price for the rest of her life. I have no doubt it was disappointment that killed her, not the awful climate, not the hardships, not the horrible tropical diseases, those she could weather manfully. But disappointment, that's more insidious: that she couldn't tackle head on in her usual fashion, that she was too stubborn to acknowledge, not to herself and especially not to us. She never said much of course, had to keep face in front of Mama. But over the years her guard would slip, and now and then the odd line or phrase in her monthly letters would let me know how disappointing her new life was, how little it matched her expectations. *At least I have my garden* she would write, or *I'd join the League too if I were home.*

I don't think Gilbert featured much in her decision to go, but his marriage proposal gave her spinning compass a direction different to the one Mama wanted. No, it wasn't about Gilbert – my sister hardly knew him when she boarded the SS Nubian, south bound for Port Natal. They had met one summer when Eleanor, sixteen at the time, had accompanied Lord and Lady What-What to Cowes as under-governess. Gilbert had just returned home from fighting Zulus in Africa. Their romance was brief, just a few weeks and a short exchange of letters, but it left Eleanor heart-broken. She didn't hear from him for almost ten years, and then, quite suddenly he wrote to her and a fresh correspondence sprang up between them. It was wrong of course, for Mama to intercept his letters – but she didn't want to see her daughter hurt again. When Eleanor discovered her perfidy, there was an awful, awful row.

Gilbert, back in Africa by then, must have been perplexed

when he didn't get a reply to his latest letter, a proposal of marriage no less, so he wrote to a mutual friend and asked him to find out why Eleanor had stopped writing. I still remember the day he came, that friend of Gilbert's. His name was Mr Clarke, Mr James Clarke.

There was a bite to the wind that made passers-by pull their coats tight about them, their hats low over their ears, as they hurried down the road. We were in the parlour, Eleanor and I. I, busy with some tapestry and she pacing up and down at the window, always restless our Eleanor. Just as I was about to ask her to settle down for pity's sake, she stopped dead still. There was a man walking up the road, glancing at a slip of paper in his hand and then at the cottages. He was not from Stratford, even I could tell that by the cut of his coat. London perhaps? Was it someone Eleanor knew? Was that why she drew behind the curtains, but kept staring out at him? The man stood just outside our house, took off his hat, smoothed down his fair hair and pulled on his sideburns. Eleanor stood immobile, but I jumped up and ran out of the room, calling to Mama that there was a visitor, a strange man at our door. I knew something was going to happen.

That was James Clarke. Eleanor introduced him to Mama as a friend she'd made in Cowes, a brother of Lucy Clarke. Mama was disapproving. She knew Gilbert was also from Cowes and must have suspected a coup. Poor Mr Clarke. He was very polite and kept up pleasantries all through a lengthy tea. When Mama finally put her cup in its saucer, he stood up and said to Eleanor;

'Shall we take a stroll, Miss Lewis?'

'A stroll? But it is bitter outside,' protested Mama.

'Just give me a moment to find my coat and hat,' Eleanor said standing. 'We won't be long Mama. Be sure to keep the fire bright Cora, and do your best to finish up that cloth.'

I clearly wasn't to think of accompanying them. Eleanor

pulled on her grey serge coat and winter bonnet, but her gloves would not behave. Here was a finger turned inside out and she had to blow into it and slap it against her thigh, but still it would not cooperate. Mr Clarke took the glove from her and righted it.

I watched them leave from the sitting room window. Eleanor had forgotten to change her boots, by the time they reached Chapel Street, her feet would be sodden. There were not many people outdoors now. Those who were scuttled past them like crabs. But Eleanor and Mr Clarke walked slowly, heads together. I watched them until they turned at the corner.

'You forget I am a person!' Eleanor shouted, barely a minute after Mr Clarke had said good-bye at the door. It was already dark by then and Papa was home, scrubbing his hands at the kitchen sink. Mama was making apple turnovers for afters and I was setting the table. It was still half set next morning.

In one of the very last letters she wrote to me herself, towards the end of 1922, shortly before she had to give up writing altogether (already her handwriting was so poor I could hardly make it out), she said she thought God was probably punishing her for the sin of insurrection, and if so, He must regard it as one of the worst sins a person can commit, for she was suffering terribly.

So perhaps I am right. Perhaps she gave up her home and her family all those years ago just to prove a point. Just to remind us all that she was a person.

Mrs Turner's theory

When Eleanor read to us, it made everything else seem like fiction. A dusk-like softness would fall across the faces before her, a softening and a slowing down, as if every gesture was in slow motion, every sound muted. Only Eleanor's voice existed. The words themselves often escaped me, but the music of them filled my ears. Eleanor's voice was like my mother's hand stroking my head, lulling my mind. Her words would loop and dive around us, tumble at our feet and swim off in the breeze. Then one morning, it was the same morning Captain Maloney announced we'd reach Port Natal within two days, Eleanor stopped reading, very abruptly, just broke off midway through a chapter.

'That is all for now, I'm afraid,' she said, more than a trifle brusquely. 'Mrs Turner, it's time for luncheon is it not?'

She'd caught me by surprise, I was far away, dreaming about summer picnics no doubt, and while I fumbled for the watch I wore pinned to my bosom, she disappeared down the gangway.

The girls were always pestering Eleanor to read to them. Jane Austen's *Pride and Prejudice* was their favourite. They wanted to know what happened to Elizabeth and Mr Darcy – the Dreadful-Mr-Darcy, as they called him. I don't think Miss Lewis, Eleanor that is, cared two jots about the lovers, she was more interested in the magazines borrowed from the Captain, but she always obliged them by reading a chapter or two before going back to her own books and magazines.

Eleanor was a tall, skinny girl with hazel eyes and a mass of dark hair she wore pulled back quite severely, in the way of a governess, and to my mind, quite unattractively. She was a plain girl though her skin was lovely, a real English rose. She wore a cerulean blue skirt, with no hint of a bustle. Her tiny waist was accentuated by a darker sash and widening skirt which flared just above the knee. I remember that outfit exactly: the white shirtwaist blouse with ever so slightly puffed sleeves and the short, matching jacket. It was the only outfit I ever saw Eleanor wearing. The rest of her trousseau went to the bottom of the ocean, as did everyone's luggage, when our ship ran ashore in the River Tagus. Every few days, one of us would stay in our cabin – we were cabin mates Eleanor and I – wrapped in a sheet, while the other would wash her set of clothing and hang it out to dry. It was the only thing we could do under the circumstances.

Eleanor was very bookish, always reading, whatever she could get her hands on, or writing in her little notebook. She seldom joined in the games or play acting, not that she was unfriendly, or melancholy, not at all, she was full of life and thrilled to be aboard, always asking the Captain questions about what she could see from deck. I preferred to keep my eyes on board ship, watching the girls' goings-on from my deck chair. Being somewhat older and already widowed, I took it upon myself to look after them.

'What a lark they are having,' I had commented to Mr Pritchard that morning. I think everyone was excited by Captain Maloney's news, excited and anxious no doubt.

'Indeed.' Mr Pritchard settled himself in a deep wicker chair, pleased I'd invited him to join me. 'It is best they enjoy themselves in the time left to them, my dear,' he said rather familiarly, as one tends to be when meeting under such transient circumstances. Having dined with us each evening since Portugal, he now spoke to me as if he had known me all my life.

'Life can be hard in the colonies, especially for a woman.'

'So I believe.'

'Do you suppose it's the lure of romance that has them south bound?'

'For grooms most of them have never met? I very much doubt it, Mr Pritchard.'

'Ah well, there are some who'd say any husband is better than none.'

'I'm afraid I simply can't agree. Given half a chance there is many a woman who would be better off on her own. But that is not possible in our great Empire, is it now, Mr Pritchard?' I said it lightly, but there was an edge to my voice.

'There, there, Mrs Turner, I didn't mean any offence.'

'All I'm saying is that if these young women had better options they would surely have taken them.' I turned my attention back to the girls who were flocking around Eleanor again. Lord knows if I had had any options I would not have been buttoned into that stuffy black dress, off to live as my brother's perpetual guest in some God-forsaken corner of the world.

Mr Pritchard leaned back in his chair and closed his eyes. The poor fool probably had no idea what to say to women with opinions of their own.

'Eleanor,' the girls beg, 'will you read to us again?'

Eleanor smiles and slips her half-written letter into a magazine and tucks it neatly into her bag. 'What about a different story?' she asks. 'I could tell you a story about an adventurer, a woman adventurer who travels to foreign places just for the sake of ....'

'No, no. We want to know what happens to Elizabeth Bennet , don't we, girls?' It's Ida – ring-leader from the start.

'Really? All right then – where were we? Ah yes, Elizabeth just refused Mr Collins.' Eleanor begins reading. But it wasn't long before she broke off. 'That's all for now, I'm afraid,' she said, more than a trifle brusquely. 'Mrs Turner, it's time for luncheon is it not?'

After lunch I went down to our cabin, knocked and entered. Eleanor was lying face down on her bunk, though she sat up very quickly, embarrassed I'd caught her all to pieces. She certainly looked a sight, her face was blotchy, eyes puffy.

'I told the girls, too much reading must have given you a headache. Do you feel a little better now?' 'Her hair, rich dark hair, had come completely undone from its usually sober bun. It made her look younger, hanging loose about her shoulders, more vulnerable. I picked up her hair brush and began brushing it.

'Tell me about this man you are going to marry,' I said after a while. 'When did you meet him?'

'In Cowes, in the summer of '83. Mr Knight, Gilbert, was home on holiday after a stint in the army. I had a day off from my duties.'

'1883. That's a long time ago.'

'Yes, yes it is. Ten years.'

'Have you seen him since, your Gilbert?'

'No.'

'Ah.' I kept on brushing her hair, long strokes from the scalp all the way to the bottom of her spine.

'He went back to Africa just after we met, adventuring. But he has a good job now as a clerk on the railways – a job with prospects.'

'And do you love him?' She was quiet for such a long time, I thought she wasn't going to answer my question. Granted it was very impertinent.

'I don't know, Mrs Turner. I liked him very much when we met, but I was just a child then. So much has happened since. The thing is ...'

'Yes?'

'The thing is I don't know if I am cut out for marriage at all.'

'Some people are cut out for marriage, my dear,' I said, 'and some are not.' There. That is what I said to her, and I still believe it. 'Very few women have the luxury to say no,' I said. 'It's not that we lack courage, but alternatives.'

That is my theory. Eleanor lacked alternatives.

Big Gladys's theory

Sometimes I think daughters know least about their mothers, or perhaps being more like them than is comfortable to recognise, we try to hide it, we become forgetful of how very like them we are. At least I am, though I think my father's gentle influence, his placid nature is part of my make up too. It was just that – that placidness of his – that annoyed my mother so. Daddy was artistic, given to day-dreaming, quite happy to sit and do nothing, or so it seemed to Mother, but really he was observing beauty, a leaf, the curve of a branch, the patterns on an emerald spotted dove, the shape-shifting shadows of the frangipani tree, the colours of the gaudy bougainvilleas. Daddy liked to sketch, he had a notebook full of beautiful drawings, but Mother, in a fit of pique, tossed it out. I don't ever remember seeing him sketch again. If he did, he did it in secret.

Eleanor, my mother, was not at all dreamy. She was matter of fact and very organised, a hard worker, tolerated no nonsense – though she loved to kiss and cuddle us, play hide and seek with us in the garden – but only when we were alone, when Daddy wasn't there. She was very clever, and wanted us to be clever too. That was all right for my brother Oliver and much later for little Will, they were naturally clever. When I reached my teens, she gave up badgering me to study harder.

'It doesn't matter much I suppose,' she said, 'women have to give up any sort of noetic life when they are married, and I dare say you will marry one day too.'

Mother seemed resentful of Daddy, not just for being placid, but for the way her life had turned out, as if it was his fault. I didn't know what noetic meant at the time, but it was clear Mother felt she had sacrificed a lot for very little. It's true she'd had a very hard life.

Mother arrived in Durban with only the clothes on her back. The very next day, in a little church on the Bluff, she married a man she had last seen ten years prior. Daddy had a house in the new suburb of Berea, and she was obliged to begin her wifely duties immediately. Just imagine, if you can, the shock of it all. Arriving in sub tropical Durban in the height of summer, every day blistering hot and pouring with rain, and Durban a small, scabby little place.

It didn't take very long, a matter of weeks in fact, before Mother was pregnant. My brother Oliver was born before the year was out, and a very sickly child he was, not at all suited to the harsh climate. Mother succumbed to tropical fevers too, and they came down with at least one very nasty bout of malaria each. Between looking after frail little Oliver, coping with her own poor health, and running the house with no mother, no sisters, no family at all to support her, life must have been very tough indeed.

And then I came along, three years later, a robust baby that didn't need (or get) the mollycoddling Oliver got. Mother always loved him most, more than anyone – including Daddy.

War broke out with the Boers - The Second Boer War that is – when I was three years old. Down in Durban we were well away from the worst of it, but then at the beginning of 1900, Daddy, who worked as a clerk for the railways, was sent up to Ladysmith, an important rail town, immediately after it was relieved from a long siege. Mother, Oliver and I followed a little while later and we all moved into a small house. It was painted black and the grounds (you cannot describe them as a garden) were still strewn with shell cases. It was only a temporary home, and as soon as something better came up we moved again, this time close to the railway station and next door to the police station.

Mother started working in the garden immediately. That was always the first thing she did whenever we had to move. One thing I can say for Natal, plants grow even when your back is turned. I remember playing in the bottom of the garden, behind one of the beds mother had planted, plants whose cascading stems were already covered with masses of huge yellow trumpet flowers. While down there I heard horses. It wasn't the sound horses usually made when they came into town, the quick, crisp clip-clop. It was a much sadder sound, and it was the sadness that made me look up. Coming along Lyle Street, was a party of bedraggled horses with even more bedraggled riders. Neither horses nor riders looked up when I called out 'Hello!'.

I heard Daddy tell Mother later that a group of Boers had come in to surrender at the police station that afternoon. 'Poor buggers,' he said. And Mother didn't even chide him.

Some years passed before we moved back to Durban. Daddy stopped going to work – there was no longer work for him to go to, no money left to run the railway. It was during this time, a time of great depression across the whole Colony, that my little brother Will was born. Though she loved him, he was a great strain on Mother who was nearly forty by then.

Daddy turned down a new job with the railways because it was of lower status than the one he'd held in Ladysmith. Mother was furious, she couldn't keep a family together on the vegetables he grew, she said. They argued a lot, but always behind closed doors. The differences between them seemed to multiply. Mother would lose herself working in the garden and Daddy in his day-dreams. It was Oliver, darling, sainted Oliver who found work first, then me. When the Second World War broke out, Mother was frantic with worry about Oliver, but he was found to be unfit and could not enlist – perhaps because of all those childhood illnesses.

A few years after the war Mother began to show signs of rheumatoid arthritis. At first it was manageable, but then she could no longer garden, no longer cook. Then she could no longer bath or dress herself, no longer write, no longer hold a book. As her pain and disability increased she began needing more and more care, so I gave up my job as a dress-maker and nursed her. For years. My poor dear Walter. When he married me, he got my parents too.

After she died, I found a small suitcase I'd never seen before. It was made of sturdy red leather and measured only five by twelve by fifteen inches. Daddy said he'd never seen it before either, so I thought it wise to open it sometime when he was out visiting. The key, well that was easy, there was a small brass key tied on a scrap of faded blue fabric in among her under-wear. I'd always wondered about that key, but had known better than to ask.

Inside the suitcase was a magazine from the Royal Geographic Society dated 1892; a newspaper clipping about a woman explorer where Mother (I presume) had underlined just one sentence; '"I could not endure a domestic lifestyle," said Miss Bird'; and a type-written note from the *Natal Herald* dated 13 August 1908, which read, 'Dear Mrs Knight. We regret to inform you, there are no vacancies for columnists at present.' My mother had entertained notions of being a writer and not one of us knew about it. There was also a thick white envelope addressed to Mr G. Knight, 13 Enfield Road, Durban, Port Natal, in Mother's hand. There was no stamp on the envelope, nor was it sealed. Inside was a letter dated 24 December 1892 – and the address given was Residencial da Opiniao do Porto, Lisbon. Mother must have stayed there when ship-wrecked.

'*My dear Gilbert*' I read with trepidation.

There is something I must tell you. It weighs heavily on my heart. I thought I should be able to live with it. I thought it better not to burden you with the truth, but there is something about surviving a ship-wreck, something about another chance at life, that makes you look at things differently.

I could not go on. I could not go on reading Mother's unsent letter. I did not want to know what had weighed so heavily on her heart. And why, if she had written it, had she not posted it? Why ever had she kept it? My always composed mother in a turmoil? My matter-of-fact mother with a dreadful secret?

I was always known as the rough, tough one – but in all truth I am a coward. Philemon was burning dry leaves in the fire pit at the bottom of the garden. It must have been May or June – the deciduous trees, jacaranda, leopard, golden trumpet, and the coral trees were all losing their leaves. I folded the pages carefully along the worn lines, and without looking down at the letter in my hands even once more, I slipped it back into its white envelope, and stood-up. Perhaps I was in shock. I walked across the lawn, past the violas, the marigolds, past the sunflowers and the zinnias, past the purple cosmos growing beneath the leafless jacaranda and down the stones steps to the fire pit. Mother's secret blackened at the edges, puckered, and then burst into flames.

I suppose you could say I don't dare have a theory.

Little Gladys's theory

I don't dabble in make-believe, I like facts, so I will only tell you what I know. The facts we have about my Grandmother Eleanor don't tell us anything about why she agreed to marry Gilbert, nor why he took ten years to propose. We don't know what she did in those years, though she'd clearly had enough of governess-ing by the end of it, and we only know a little of what Gilbert was up to. The only certain thing is that a correspondence ensued between them, and towards the end of 1892, he asked her to come out to Durban and marry him. She must still have been fond enough of him to say yes.

Gilbert, my Granddad, first went to South Africa as a member of the 60th Foot, King's Royal Rifle Corps. Why he joined the army was always a bit of a mystery. As far as I can tell, though he never confessed this to me himself, he had been involved in a fight with some chap who had insulted his girlfriend. The police were called, and Gilbert spent the night in jail. Next morning, unable to face his father, he fled to the army. Some months later, two hundred men were needed to go to Africa, to Isandhlwana, where the British Army were preparing to go into battle against the Zulus again. One February morning, their Colonel said: 'Let any men who wish to go, take one step to the front.'

Apparently, all eight hundred men stepped forward. Granddad said it was one of the most thrilling moments of his life. They sailed at the end of that same month ... ten thousand men in all. It was 1879.

The English made short work of the Zulus and troops were out of Zululand by September, except for some, including Granddad. And he was still there when the First Boer War broke out. Granddad survived Majuba, left as part of a small regiment at the bottom of the hill to guard lines of communication while the rest of the troops climbed to their deaths.

The following year, his sister died, and Granddad, who had been in and out of hospital with various diseases and was by this time sick too of being a soldier, wrote and asked his father to buy him out of the army, which his father duly did. He worked his passage home aboard a ship, and that is how he, Gilbert Knight came to be in Cowes, the summer of 1883.

Eleanor died before I was born. Though Granddad said very little about their meeting, I do remember him describing their first kiss, 'Aah! Nectar!' is what he said. But whatever he felt for Eleanor at the time, it wasn't sufficient to keep him in the home country. Africa was in his blood, and he left again just a few months later.

Once back in Natal, he took on all sorts of jobs. He was overseer of a road-making gang on Town Hill, Pietermaritzburg, and then a clerk for an accountant, before moving to Johannesburg. It was there he became engaged to a Miss Ferguson, but only for a short while. It seems he ended the arrangement somewhat abruptly on discovering something questionable about her moral standing. Perhaps because of this, he moved on to the Cape Colony, where he lived in quarters in the Castle, and worked as a civilian clerk for the military. Next he took a job in a law firm, again as a clerk. Eventually he returned to Natal, (preferring its clime and natives to the Cape's) where he became a clerk with the Natal Government Railway in Durban.

No guesses or theories. That's all I know.

Sandra's theory

Have you ever heard of Nellie Bly? She was so determined not to be confined to writing about gardening, fashion or food that she spent ten days in a mad house so she could write an article about it for the New York World in 1887. In 1889 she travelled around the world in seventy two days, six hours, eleven minutes and fourteen seconds – a record-breaking trip.

Have you heard of Isabella Lucy Bird? In 1889 her father gave her one hundred pounds and told her she could travel until she had spent it all. Isabella Lucy Bird visited India, Tibet, Persia, Kurdistan and Turkey. She stayed and stayed and stayed, adding to her income by writing travel articles. She reportedly said, this Isabella Lucy Bird, 'I cannot endure a domestic lifestyle'.

Have you heard of Mary French Sheldon? If not, Google her too. American born, she moved to London in 1876. In 1891 she left, not only to explore East Africa, but to explore it alone (being the 1890s – alone meant without other Europeans). 'For what good?' she was asked, and 'Whatever prompted you?' Her answer? 'My interests lie outside the limitations of women's legitimate province.'

My great-grandmother Eleanor Knight, nee Lewis, had heard of them. I have her red leather suitcase, and in it I found an old Royal Geographical Society magazine which had a piece on Isabella Lucy Bird; several newspaper articles by Nellie Bly about her round-the-world trip (which one of Eleanor's American cousins must have sent her) and an advertisement for Mary French Sheldon's book, entitled, *Sultan to Sultan: Adventures among the Masai and other tribes of east Africa.*

Perhaps I am guilty of projection, given my own love of travel. Perhaps I am guilty of making things up. I like to make things up. But my theory is this: Eleanor wanted to see the world, and Gilbert with all his stories of adventure, so far away across the seas in 'deepest-darkest-Africa', was the best ticket she had.

For Your Own Good

There is nothing wrong with the new apartment in Sea Point. Nothing she can lay a finger on. Nothing she can point to. The front door opens onto a lounge, dining room, and open plan kitchenette (in pale pinks and blue). There is a large window above the kitchen sink that catches the morning sun, and sliding doors onto a small west-facing balcony with a view of the ocean. The main bedroom is a good size and has a wall of built in cupboards with an off-white pearly finish. The second room is somewhat smaller, but still big enough for her children when they visit, one at a time. When they are not visiting (which is most of the time) it could be a work room, a place to write letters, do puzzles, dry her personals. The bathroom with its non-slip bath and shower, and hand rails at all the places she may need them, is conveniently situated between the two rooms. No, there isn't anything wrong exactly, but she likes nothing about it.

Andrew has already, it seems, made up his mind. And Lisa is right behind him, thinks Joan, egging him on the way she used to when they were little. The two of them together had always made a formidable front.

Joan is tired, very tired. She wishes he would leave. Not just her room, not just the hospital, but the country. Wishes he would get back on the plane, 'thank you very much for the visit, darling', and leave her alone.

She watches him through half-closed eyes, sitting there in the leatherette Lazy Boy with another clutch of documents in his hands. His head has the look of a moulting animal about it. His cheeks have gone flabby, his neck puggish in the expensive collared shirts he wears. Middle-age does not suit Andrew. Not in looks, nor demeanour. The gentle boyishness, the easy charm ... gone. All that's left is the bully.

'Just think, Ma. No more cooking. You can eat in the dining room everyday. The medical facilities are world class, and the club offers all sorts of activities. There is quite a social programme on offer; movies, concerts, outings, games evenings, pottery classes, even dancing. You can make new friends there.' Andrew sounds remarkably like the promotional video the Atlantica salesman (no, not salesman, lifestyle consultant) had shown them. 'And a twenty-four hour concierge service. You won't have to worry about a thing there.'

What he means is that he won't have to worry about a thing, with me in a place like that. That Lisa won't have to worry either. Joan is not fooled. 'I don't need twenty-four hour service.'

'Besides the house is too big for you to manage any more. And it's looking really dilapidated. Needs a lot more than a coat of paint, you do realise that, don't you? It would take a fortune to renovate. I'm surprised the neighbours haven't complained.'

Actually the neighbours have complained. But not about the house. It's a bit of a joke in her street really, old Mrs StClair and her late night music. Joan thinks fondly of her classical music club, but says nothing. The partial collapse of her lung has left her short of breath and with a relentless pain in her chest.

Andrew picks up the remote and flicks to the golf. 'You could've broken your neck, never mind your hip. Why didn't you send Xolile up the ladder, that's what he's there for, isn't he? And all for some bloody pears.' He's muttering now.

Joan remembers how she'd caught Andrew sitting in that same pear tree pelting passers-by with the soft fruit.

'Next time it could be worse. You could have a heart attack. Or a stroke or something. What would you do then, all on your own? Sydney is not just around the corner and ...' Andrew glances up at his mother. For a moment, just the briefest of moments, he remembers what it was like to snuggle in bed beside her, the way she curved her long body to make a cave for him. What was that rhyme she would murmur? 'I love this boy like a rabbit loves to run ...'

Andrew looks away, looks back at the contract on his lap. She would never concede to something like this if she was up and about. Perhaps he and Lisa should back off? No. The time has come. It's for her own good.

Andrew moves fast. The following day he signs the paperwork for Atlantica; gives Pam Golding sole mandate to sell number thirteen (it will be snapped up in no time); contracts Stuttafords Removal Company to pack up the house; and arranges temporary security measures with WatchDog. He consults his mother's doctor; speaks to the matron at Atlantica; and makes arrangements for Joan's transfer from hospital to the recovery centre. She won't manage on her own for at least six weeks, maybe longer. He can't possibly stay that long, can't even stay another six days. He has to move fast.

Joan pulls her duvet higher. It is unthinkable to her that she will never go home again. It is unthinkable that this is what her children think best for her. That she no longer has it in her to stand up to them. Atlantica Retirement Resort: just the name of it makes her lips pucker.

A nurse comes in to check her pulse, temperature and blood pressure. She shifts the support beneath Joan's hip into a different position, fiddles with the drip feeding her pain-killers and antibiotics, adjusts the tubes draining her lung. 'Feeling any better, sweetie?' she asks. 'Need to wee-wee?'

Andrew wants her to decide on things now, and when she won't, or can't, he does. He makes lists on his iPad. Things for Lisa. Thing for him. He chooses small, non-breakable, items he can take on the plane: some of his father's books, the Pierneef etching of Chapman's Peak, Dawid Botha's oil painting of a fisherman's cottage (frames to be removed), the gold clock from the mantelpiece, the Chinese paperweight and a pair of silver candlesticks. His mother's fur stole and some diamanté jewellery for his (second) wife.

'And now things for your new apartment.' He sits next to her hospital bed, and reads the list he has drawn up: bed, bedside table (only one), the floral covered lounge suite from the sun-room (smaller than the living room suite), four antique chairs from the dining room and the stinkwood table from the entrance hall ('It will do as a dining room table, don't you think?'), the two smaller Persian carpets, display cabinet, red velvet chaise lounge, television, decoder, DVD player and her writing desk. Two outdoor chairs and a little table for her verandah. He lists the few kitchenware items he thinks essential ('You'll probably eat most of your meals in Atlantica's dining room'), the pictures (the Tinus de Jongh series), paintings (the Rene Le Roux will fit perfectly behind the couch), and photographs (of children and grandchildren mostly) that will make the apartment feel like home.

'It will be ready by the time you get there, I've got it all organised. The rest ...' he casts his hands out as if all her belongings were piled before him, 'will have to go. They won't fit in your new place and I can't heave them back to Australia with me.'

Joan eyes are steady, her eye-brows pulled down at the sides in a look he remembers well. She says just one word. 'Storage!' It is a command.

'Okay, okay,' Andrew concedes. It's simpler for him to organise anyway. Let Lisa deal with it when she comes over at Christmas, he thinks.

Dear Val

Thank you for your lovely letters. Of course we could Skype or email, Andrew saw to all the 'essentials' as he calls them, but I do so love a real letter ... even short ones like ours. Of course I understand you can't leave John, so don't worry about it. Husbands must take priority and I am managing fine on my own. I can't tell you how good it is to be mobile again and able to do everything for myself. Whenever the weather permits (and we've had some dreadfully wet Cape winter days) I'm even managing little walks along the Promenade. As you predicted, there is nothing like walking to lift the spirits. I do miss number thirteen dreadfully. But there you are. Everyone says moving is a great upheaval and takes time to adjust. Andrew did a relatively good job of furnishing the flat, but frankly I wish he had left it to me. I keep looking for things and then think, ah yes that must be in storage I suppose.

Your loving sister

Joan

Dear Val

An inventory is an excellent idea. How silly of me not to have thought of that for myself. I called StoreSecure immediately and they promised to send one straight away. I am still waiting — two days later.

Brenda took me for a drive past number thirteen yesterday. I wish she hadn't. They've all but knocked it down, and worse still, taken out my pear tree. From the architect's board it seems they are planning to build four units on the property, the tree must have been in the way of one of them.

Dear Val

Despite StoreSecure's assurance that the mix up is only administrative, I am growing more and more worried they've

*lost what's most precious to me. It really is the only item I
care about – and they can't quite 'locate' it. Surely it is either
there or it isn't? Andrew thinks I'm panicking unnecessarily,
but has agreed to do what he can from his side. To think
he never checked the inventory at the time! He's usually
meticulous about any sort of paperwork.*

*I'm glad to hear John is making steady progress. Do give
him my love. You can be quite glad you didn't come down
when planned, it's been a frightfully cold winter thus far.
Early summer is a much better idea. I look forward to it
tremendously.*

*Dearest Val
Just a quick note because I couldn't get you on the phone
and wanted to tell someone straight away. I have just been
appointed the new piano teacher at the Massimo School of
Music! Yes – I am to start work again. You are probably
only a little more surprised than I am. Without my house
and garden to keep me busy, time has been hanging heavy
on my hands, and you know I can't abide being idle. I also
can't bring myself to join the awful 'club' and go about here
there and everywhere with a bunch of oldies. So when I saw
the advertisement in the local Atlantic Sun, I thought why
not?! It is a temporary appointment while the regular teacher
is on maternity leave, so if I find it too much, I'll only have
to manage for three months. The school is situated in a lovely
old Victorian house, an easy walking distance from here. And
more importantly, I have the use of a wonderful Bösendorfer –
it is in really good condition. How I miss my own piano.*

★

Julian chose Sea Point because it had always been there, on the
fringe of his childhood. He chose it because although Cape
Town was 'home', he was unlikely to actually know anyone

living in Sea Point. It's not a family kind of place, not the sort of place you want to raise kids. Men his age mostly had kids, though of course they might well be grown by now.

Julian chose the house in Gordon Street between client meetings. It has everything he needs: kitchen, living room, bedroom, bathroom with shower and a small courtyard at the back. The lease agreement was straightforward, and he'd asked Nicky to deal with the agent. She would also organise things with the movers. That would be the last thing she did for him as his personal assistant.

Julian chooses a cigarette in the courtyard rather than watch the men wrestle furniture and boxes into the house. The sun has only just pushed over the rim of Signal Hill, dappling the mossy paving. Grover Washington sits near him, his focus on a little stop-start lizard. He wonders how long the cat will stay, how long the lizard will live. Julian can't see the sea, but he can hear it above the traffic in Main Road and the voices in his new house.

'We're finished, Meneer. You sure you want everything in the lounge? We can carry things upstairs if you like?'

'Everything is fine as it is. Thank you,' says Julian, without looking at what they've done. He takes the clipboard and signs his name in the blank spaces the man in a Stuttafords' overall points to, then follows him into the kitchen and towards the front door. Boxes line the wall, J. StClair written in big black letters on them. Two Morris chairs stand side-by-side, and a worn leather couch fills the bay window. In the middle of the living room is an enormous piano. Julian stops in his tracks.

He should have said something straight away.

Julian wakes up. His back is stiff from sleeping on the couch and there is a bad taste in his mouth. Whiskey and cigarettes? Too much garlic in the Woolies lasagne? He shifts onto his back and lies quietly, listening to the noises in the street.

The little beeps of car alarms being deactivated, the bang of doors, high heels against the tar, voices, irritated mostly, and hurried. The sound of engines starting, the swish of tyres on a wet road. There is not much between them; a cement pavement, a leggy plumbago hedge, the glass and brick of his front wall. Everyone, it seems, leaves at once and Gordon Street is quiet again.

Julian is alone, except for Grover Washington and the bergie who pokes around the rubbish bins, hopeful of left-overs or serviceable throw outs. Julian knows he'll be there today, is probably there already, because it's Thursday, rubbish day. He knows the man's name is Gordon, like the street. They are on first name terms, he and Gordon. Both of them homeless, though Julian has a roof over his head.

He gets up from the couch, walks past the boxes and goes into the kitchen, puts on the kettle and spoons Nescafe into last night's mug. Sonja got the espresso machine. 'If there is anything I miss,' he says to the cat, 'it's the espresso machine.'

Julian looks at his watch. Usually by this time he is already on site, or with clients, or in meetings with contractors or engineers. But Julian doesn't have a job to go to. He is taking a break. That's what his friends in Durban said he should do.

'You need to take a break, buddy, get out of here.' Karl was a good friend. 'For your own good.' Then, a week later he'd said, 'Are you sure you know what you doing? Moving to Cape Town? That's radical, bro. What I meant was, go on holiday ... a surf trip, or climb Kilimanjaro, or something. What about your job? Are you sure you shouldn't think this over, when you're not so stressed?'

In the bathroom Julian washes his face, feeling it bristle under his hands. He squeezes a generous amount of Palmolive Shaving Cream into his palm and works up a lather before unwrapping a disposable razor. The bristles are days (weeks?) old, the blade nasty. Julian slices himself just under the chin. In the mirror, he sees the sudden blood scarlet against the creamy foam. He stares at his face in the mirror. Sorry bastard, he thinks, pull yourself together.

In the small cling-wrapped pile of clothes from the laundry he finds underwear and an ironed shirt. His black jeans don't show the grime. He wears wine-maker boots, brown ones. His other shoes must be in a box somewhere. Another feeble excuse not to go for a run.

Julian goes back downstairs, sits at the piano and lifts the lid. The ivories are sulky yellow. This baby must be old. He runs his fingers gently over the keys, hears Vassily Primakov play Chopin's piano concerto and wonders how long it took him to get that good, or if he was born a maestro? It had been the first concert Julian had been to in ages.

Julian walks along Main Road till he reaches Al Frascatti, run by an Italian couple. The old man never smiles or greets him, but brings a double espresso and plain omelette without Julian having to ask. The ciabatta is served with olive oil, not butter. All the tables are full. It's noisy. He feels better for being among people. There are two women at the window counter next to him. They look Sonja's age, more or less, but wear more make-up than she ever did.

'I thought Steve was going to platz!' the blonde says to her friend. 'I thought he was going to kill Ash, he was so angry.'

'Oh my God Laura, poor you. Poor Steve. But it could be worse, you know. It could've been drugs. Remember my cousin Michelle? Her daughter's in rehab again, only seventeen you know, and that's not all ...'

Laura is not really paying attention. She doesn't want sympathy and is annoyed her story is being outdone. In the window she can see the reflection of a middle-aged man sitting at the counter on the other side of Tracey. His face is plump, quite puffy actually, and his nose is large, like a Greek, she thinks, but otherwise good looking enough. There is a tiny cut on the side of his neck. His thick hair is greying and in need of a good cut. It stands up in spikes, though not the kind made on purpose. Laura knows that, she used to be a hair stylist before marrying Steve.

Laura nods at Tracey, says 'Mhmm.' But she's thinking about running her hands through this man's hair, touching the back of his neck. She is talking to him, from behind, about what style he fancies. That's how she'd met Steve, in her salon, talking about the style he fancied.

The man in the reflection is not wearing a wedding band. Laura hasn't lost the habit of looking for wedding bands, yet. He is wearing a turquoise open necked shirt with a kind of paisley pattern. His arms are heavy in the sleeves, muscular or just chubby, she can't tell. Laura sighs and smooths her shirt over her flat stomach, looks down admiringly at her cleavage and the trim bod below. Not bad for forty-five hey? she thinks.

Julian finishes the *Cape Times* and picks up the *Atlantic Sun*. He tries to ignore the woman with her bottle blonde hair and ridiculously erect tits staring at him in the reflection. The local headlines are about a new sewer pipe the Council plans to lay from Granger Bay, just north of the lighthouse. Julian remembers the lighthouse and the foghorn from when he was a kid. It used to blare out *baaap* whenever the sea mists were too thick for ships to see the shore line as they headed for Table Bay Harbour. Back then, before GPS.

Julian flips through the paper. There is an article about what to do with the stadium, something about tourists at the Waterfront, crime statistics for the area, a new deal with taxi owners. On page five, there is a picture of a group of kids standing next to a grand piano that catches his eye. It looks a little like his. Next to the photo is a small notice welcoming Mrs Joan StClair, the new piano teacher, to the school. It's not a common surname, but there are no Joans in his family that he knows of. Julian tears the notice from the paper and puts it in his pocket.

He leaves the right amount of money and a generous tip under his plate, nods to Roberto and Rosa on his way out, and leaves.

'Such a sad man,' Rosa says to her husband, watching Julian jaywalk between the taxis, buses and cars already bumper to bumper along the narrow road.

Julian walks along Main Road heading towards the city. It's a long way, he could hop onto any number of buses or taxis, but prefers to walk. It's the moment Table Mountain first comes into view that makes it so worthwhile. For blocks it's hidden by Signal Hill, ugly buildings crawling up its slopes, the tiny military base he can just make out by the white flag poles, and above it all the road, a ribbon cutting into a grey-green coat of vegetation.

Julian stands at the corner of Main and Glengariff, waiting for the light. It's the edge of Sea Point, the beginning of Green Point and urban renewal. Through the old blue gums lining the street, Julian can see the stadium looming like the shell of a giant sea urchin. The surrounding area has been well designed. He knows some of the architects and landscapers from varsity days. The other side of the road hasn't had the same attention, though there are a whole lot of new eateries that have been nicely done up. The light changes and Julian crosses the road thinking he might give Mrs J. StClair a call.

Julian avoids the dog turds and McDonalds packets that strew the pavement. An old woman in a maroon dressing gown shuffles along behind her poodle. A prostitute, Nigerian possibly, gives him the once over and returns to filing her nails. Julian wonders what makes him look such an unlikely client. He passes a group of kids in school uniform, heavy bags slung over their shoulders, talking loudly, half Xhosa, half English. They seem to be in no hurry. Arriving late? Leaving early? Playing hooky? He can't tell.

A man and a woman brush past, intent on their conversation.

Their perfumes are shrill, he can smell them long after they have turned into a coffee shop. He passes advertisements for penis enlargements, pain-free abortions and Jesus (Have *you* given your life to the Lord?) posted on walls, street-light poles, post boxes, and empty windows. As Julian draws level with the Traffic Department, he looks up to the right. There it is – Table Mountain.

By the time he reaches the City Hall, Julian is pooped. He leans against the sandstone wall, rolls a cigarette nimbly between forefinger and thumb, an old skill he's not forgotten. Two street kids come up and ask for money. He shakes his head, looks away. The street is full of people walking to or from the Parade, or the station. It's the busy end of town, the African end of town. Why did he come here?

The kids move closer. 'Agmangiveustheskuifthenbaas-assebliefmanmybaas.'

Julian takes a drag, exhales and hands it over. He reaches into his pocket and gives them a fifty rand note. Enough for a lolly, he thinks, taking in the dilated pupils, the bony wrists and elbows, the way their words run into each other. Or a burger and chips.

Julian used to go to classical concerts at the City Hall with his granny, she'd make him wear a tie. He'd loved them, the concerts, loved the music and the display of musicians. Dressed all in black, they looked like tok-tokkies from up there on the balcony. But Julian thinks of himself more as a jazz man now. He listens to Abdullah Ibrahim, Basil 'Manenberg' Coetzee, Miriam Makeba, Dave Brubeck, Billie Holiday and the rest. He does love movies about classical music though, *Amadeus*, *Mr Holland's Opus*, *The Piano*, *Shine* – they were his favourites, especially *The Piano*. He saw that three times, though Sonja wouldn't go with him. Not even once.

Julian could go to a coffee shop. He could call up one of his old Cape Town buddies and see if anyone is free for lunch. As far as he knows Greg still has offices on Dunkley Square. Nah, he doesn't feel like telling the whole boring story, putting up with the show of sympathy, the jokes, the 'Mandy and I would love to have you round for supper ... some (other) time.' Besides, he hasn't even let anyone know he's back in town, though most likely word's out – Sonja probably posted it on Facebook weeks ago.

He sits on the main stairs of the City Hall in a slice of pale winter sun, pulls out the newspaper cutting and reads it again. Then he takes out his mobile (there are two more messages from Karl) and types in the number. After the phone rings a few times, it cuts to an answering machine.

'Hello,' he says, 'this is Julian StClair. I am phoning about piano lessons. For a beginner.' He leaves his number, then hangs up.

There is music coming from across the road now, from somewhere on the Parade. Julian walks over to get a closer look. A group of musicians, not a full orchestra, but a good collection of violinists, cellists, wind instruments and even a piano, are giving a free performance, donations welcome. Julian makes his way towards the piano. The girl behind it, twenty perhaps, has long dark hair spilling out of the rough knot she's tied it in at the nape of her neck. She has a small earring in her nose and wears patterned leggings under a short denim skirt. Her purple shirt is half unbuttoned and he can see a leopard print vest under its thin fabric. He closes his eyes against the look of her and concentrates on the music, as she is.

When the concert ends, Julian puts a two hundred rand note in the hat, and heads back towards Sea Point.

Julian takes the route past Greenmarket Square, where traders try to sell him curios from Zimbabwe, Zambia, Mozambique, Angola. He looks at the clock on Inn on the Square – it's only mid-afternoon, still hours to fill. At Sturk's Tobacconists on Shortmarket Street, he buys more Rizla and another packet of

Drum, then adds a packet of Boxer for Gordon. Outside, he waits for a delivery van and a scooter to pass before crossing, their wheels *wadawadawada-ering* across the cobblestones.

Boardmans is still where it used to be. Julian wanders up and down the aisles until a young shop assistant with faultless skin, full lips and a perfectly straight nose corners him near the electrical appliances.

'Anything particular I can help you with, sir?' The man is not as young as he first appears. There are lines around his eyes and at the corner of his mouth that widen as he smiles. 'Nothing? Nothing at all? Shopping for a present? For your girlfriend, or wife perhaps?'

Julian shakes his head. 'I need an espresso machine. That's all.'

'A single, or double? Can I recommend the double?' The assistant leads the way down the aisle, 'You never know when you might need it – even if you're single.' The man's laugh is tinny. Julian tries not to let the joke sting. He realises it's one the man's cracked hundreds of times before.

'They come in a stainless steel finish, or in just about any colour combo you can imagine, but, unfortunately, we only have red or steel left at this very moment.'

Julian points to the stainless steel model. 'Single,' he says.

Julian feels ridiculous. He has a long walk ahead and now also a large bag to carry. Why on earth did he do that? The machine he didn't intend to buy is heavy. As soon as he reaches Strand Street, Julian hops onto a taxi heading for Sea Point.

Gordon Street is empty. Grover is waiting for him. So is the piano. He lifts the lid and props it open so he can admire the insides. Then he plays Beethoven's *Moonlight Sonata* on his iPod as loud as he can, while letting his hands run up and down the keyboard. The music finishes and Julian gets up to pour himself a whiskey, sits down again and tries out the first few notes.

When his mobile rings, he checks to see who it is. Unknown. Julian puts the phone back next to the keyboard, then snatches it up again, suddenly remembering his call to the music school. 'Julian, hello.'

'This is Joan,' says an elderly voice, 'Joan StClair. I'm phoning from the Massimo School of Music. You're interested in piano lessons, I believe?' Joan tries hard to keep the warble from her voice. 'For a beginner your message said, how old is the child?'

'It's for me. I mean, I want to learn to play the piano myself.'

'Oh. Oh I see.' There is a longish pause. 'Have you any experience, ever played before?'

'No, never. No experience. But I have just, er, acquired a piano, and thought I should learn to play it. My father was very musical. So was his father. They always said it ran in the StClair family.' Julian is aware that he's talking a lot, but hell, how to explain the situation? It's not like the piano actually belongs to him.

'Yes. Yes it is. So ... the lessons are for you.' Joan says. As far as she knows all the pupils at Massimo's are school children, still nobody explicitly said she shouldn't take on adults. But honestly, they are the devil to teach.

'What kind of piano?' she asks, stalling.

'Steinway & Sons.' Julian runs his thumb over the gilt letters.

'Really? Gosh. That is something special.'

'It's a Grand',

'Oh?'

'Concert size, I think. I've been reading up about them on the internet.'

Joan smiles, sure he must be exaggerating. 'Well if it is, it's a remarkable piano indeed,' she says. 'Goodness me. There weren't many of those in the country in my day. You are very fortunate.' Or maybe just a crank? she thinks.

'Do you have space for another pupil? I can come mornings or afternoons. We could make it on a trial basis if you prefer, say three or four lessons to begin with? Then you can decide if you see your way clear to keep me on.' Now that he has her on the phone, Julian is determined not to let her go until she agrees, at least to that much.

Joan and Julian schedule a class for Thursday, three thirty. The School is busy on a Thursday afternoon, it would be quite safe, if he is a crank. And if he doesn't turn up, she hasn't lost anything. She warns him not to expect too much. And how odd they should have the same surname.

Julian takes a sip of whiskey, then places the glass back carefully on a piece of newspaper so as not to spoil the piano's patina. He hums while trying, over and over, to get the opening notes right. Tomorrow he'll buy a big flat screen TV and DVD player. Mr Video is just down the road – they're sure to have *The Piano* or *Shine* on their shelves. He could watch them both, back to back, after he's gone for a run, no-one to complain or suggest he fixes the cupboard handles instead. Maybe I should make a start unpacking those boxes tonight, he thinks, bending down to pick up Grover, and I should really let Karl know I'm doing okay.

Joan walks slowly back to Atlantica. The days are starting to get a little longer, she can take her time without worrying about it getting too dark. She greets Norman-the-Doorman, then takes the lift up to the ninth floor apartment she might yet call home. She unlocks the door and flicks on the lights, walks across the room to her television and picks up the photo of herself. There she is, dressed in a ball gown, hair up in a chignon, large diamanté dangling from each ear and draped around her throat. In her left arm is a large bouquet of carnations, and beside her, holding her right hand in his white-gloved fingers, is Otto Klemperer himself. But Joan is not looking at the famous conductor, nor even at the woman she was. She is looking at the piano in the photograph, her piano. A Steinway & Sons Concert Grand.

They'd better track it down and soon, she thinks.

Thicker Than Water

All Queenstown has come to see them off. The Mayor and his Relief Committee are lost among the jubilant well wishers crowding the platform. The Town Guard plays 'God Save the King'.

'We're going home,' calls out a child suddenly, dancing about in the aisle, and the quiet in the carriage bursts. There is a hubbub of women's voices; talking, sobbing, even singing. It is March 1902.

'Home,' Isabella says to Ian, who laughs because she laughs, then presses his face back to the window as the train jolts forward. What does he know of home? she thinks. A worn, bell-shaped canvas tent? A bath house, camp kitchen? Too young to remember the little house (number nine) left behind when they fled Johannesburg with the other Uitlanders. She smooths down Ian's hair, looks over his head and out the window. The refugee camp is behind them, on the other side of town. She will never see it again.

Isabella watches Queenstown creep past. St Michael's magnificent square tower rising above the town. Their own St Columbus (the Kirk, as George always called it) away in the background. There's where Market Building and Town Hall would be on Cathcart Street. There is the bakery, oh and there is Mr Spencer and his boys, waving.

'Look Ruthie, look Ian, there is Mr Spencer, the baker. Remember how he used to bring us sugar buns on Sundays? Right in the beginning ... before food became so scarce? No?'

Ian tries to shake his head and wave wildly at the same time. The result makes the grown-ups around him laugh.

'He was just a baby then,' says old Mrs Goldberg, 'he cannot possibly remember.'

'Fancy that,' says her husband. 'Fancy remembering that, such a long time ago. What we wouldn't give for a sugar bun now, eh lad?'

'Good-bye, dear Mr Spencer. Good-bye. And thank you for the buns,' says Isabella, waving. They pass a last scattering of buildings, a few small tin-roofed houses, and that: that would be the outer ring of defence. Isabella wonders how they put so much faith in a few mounds of earth, trenches and sandbags. Would they have made a difference had the Boers come any closer? 'Goodbye Bowerskop. Good-bye Longhill. We're going home.'

The mountains lapping the north side of town are covered in all shades of Tamboekie thorn yellow. Slowly, slowly, the train pulls them away from Longhill's protective arm. Isabella would never forget any of it.

The Goldbergs, as wrinkled both of them as a school boy's sock, and their spinster niece, Ruthie, sit opposite Isabella. They have the seats to themselves, right at the end of the last carriage, just before the guard-van.

'Second class is not so bad. Not as bad as the cattle trucks we came in, eh?' says Mrs Goldberg looking around the carriage. 'Not so cramped, either. Though a sleeping coach would have been better for a 500 mile trip.'

'Look what I've got,' Ruthie says to Ian, cupping something in her large hands, lifting one work -roughened finger to make a peep hole. Ian slides off Isabella's lap.

'Is it something to eat, Miss Ruthie?' he asks.

Across the aisle sit the Harris family. Three girls in their too-short, washed out frocks and pinafores, no socks in their boots, turn away from the window. Isabella smiles at them.

'Mother, we're hungry,' clamours the largest girl, 'starving hungry.'

'What already? But we have only just started,' Mrs Harris says. 'I don't know how in heaven's name I'm going to feed you lot when we get home. Such appetites.' She scratches about in her carpet bag and takes out their food-parcel. 'I suppose this is a special occasion. Let's see what we have here.'

Ian looks up from Miss Ruthie's game at the first sound of paper crinkling, watches, but doesn't say a word.

'Sandwiches.'

There's a familiar, dusty smell, sweetish even. Isabella won't turn her head to look. She hears the girls chewing their coarse oat bread. There is no more chattering. Mrs Goldberg looks round the carriage humming to herself ... Beethoven's *Fleur-de-lis*. Mr Goldberg has his hat tilted over his eyes.

Should Isabella open her parcel too? Perhaps she could share just one sandwich with Ian now? Pretend it's ham, not horse meat? No, better to save them till later. Who knows how long the journey across the Orange Free State will take, or when next she'll get more? Besides, she notices, Ian is back to his game.

'Is it a ball?' he asks.

If we're lucky, Isabella thinks, George will have found some kind of work already, and surely, food will be easier to come by?

'Is it a frog? It is a frog! Mother, Miss Ruthie has a frog.'

'Who's she?' Mrs Goldberg leans forward suddenly and taps Isabella on the knee with a gloved hand, the stitching coming apart at the finger tips. She jerks her head in a sideways direction. Opposite Mrs Harris sits a woman in a dark cloak too heavy for the weather. Her dress is black, her boots polished. Isabella can't see much of her face, just a smooth expanse of cheek and a sharp chin protruding from under the brim of her large, black bonnet, bent towards the babe in her arms.

Nobody I recognise either, thinks Isabella, emptying out her mental pockets, trying to remember all the women she's helped during their confinement in the past three years.

'Mr Goldberg heard there might be Boers on the train. Overheard one of the committee saying so while queuing for our food-parcel,' says Mrs Goldberg.

'More likely just someone lodging in town. Lots of women did.' Isabella whispers back, then closes her eyes, grateful for the noise of the train. She will not be drawn into Mrs Goldberg's prejudices. But Mrs Goldberg is not to be dissuaded.

'Why, Mrs Harris,' she says loudly, 'I am sorry to interrupt your dinner, but you haven't introduced us to your companion yet. You must be Mrs ...?'

'Not with us,' says Mrs Harris, from behind a hand covering a mouth full of bread.

The woman in the black hat looks up. 'Morgan. Mrs Graham Morgan.' She sounds like someone clearing their throat of an annoying crumb, the 'gr' and 'g' gravelly, the 'n' heavy, drawn out.

'Ha!' says Mrs Goldberg, settling back into her seat, eyes saying I told you so. 'Ha! As if the Bittereinders out there aren't bad enough, we have a Boer in our carriage.'

'We're quite safe, my dear, quiet safe,' Mr Goldberg says patting her arm, 'block-houses all the way.'

'This monstrous war is over, Mrs Goldberg,' says Isabella firmly, 'and everyone here has suffered. I'm very sorry for your loss, Mrs Morgan, Reverend Morgan was a fine man.' Isabella turns her eyes on Mrs Harris, then Ruthie, then back to the Goldbergs. Everyone in camp knew young Reverend Morgan. Mrs Goldberg picks at the holes in her glove, looks out the window. The train begins its ascent.

Ian climbs onto Isabella's lap, and tugs at her sleeve. 'Look Mother. It's a frog,' he says.

Despite the warm berg wind blowing in through the open windows, Mrs Morgan pulls her cloak tighter about her, and rocks her baby back and forth, back and forth. Isabella feels her own body rock with the sway of the train. How her past and her future are tethered together by this track and the clackety-clack of the wheels, the dust, soot and the smoke. For the whole of Isabella's life, whether in Scotland or in Africa, in the Colonies or in the Republic, there have always been railways, the making of railways.

She can hear now, in the engine's whine, the whistle blowing on either side of her father's shift. She can hear in the train's rumble, the shouts of men, dust covered and sweating as they work the line. She can hear them grunt and curse as they hoist rock for her father's pride, the Vyfboogbrug. Yes, there had always been bridges, tunnels, tracks and tents, always been rough working men. Like the Boers, and the Uitlanders – English, Scottish, German, Portuguese, and the Africans too, who built Kruger's line across the Lowveld. She had nursed them all.

Isabella thinks of the Boers she tended back then, when her father was foreman and she the only nurse for hundreds of miles. How many of them still alive? How many Englishmen had they killed? Isabella watches a curve of track shimmer in the last of the day's sun, then disappear behind them. She cannot know what Mrs Morgan is thinking. Cannot know that their journeys move in opposite ways. That she is on an inbound journey, the other on an out.

The train pulls into a station, more siding really, no proper platform. Nobody dares get off; there is no station master to inquire how long they will be stopping. There is nobody about at all. Isabella gives Ian a drink of water, wishes it was milk.

'Dreadful place this Stormberg,' says Mr Goldberg looking at the mountains all around them. 'It will be dark before we reach Burgersdorp, that is for certain.'

The Harris girls play cat's cradle with a piece of grubby string. They have Ian entranced.

'This is the cradle,' Sarah says, 'and this one is called fish-in-a-dish. And this is the soldier's bed.'

'It is almost time for bed,' says Mrs Harris. 'Put that string back in your boot, Alice.'

Ian climbs back onto Isabella's lap and whispers 'I'm hungry' into her ear. She breaks a sandwich in half and lets him chose which piece he wants. He really looks more like his uncle Malcolm than his own father, she thinks.

There is one Boer Isabella remembers in particular, what was his name? A man who reminded her of her brother Malcolm. It was the way he recited poetry, like Malcolm could, though this man recited poets she hadn't heard of before, Boer poets. She can't remember the poems themselves, only the sounds of them, the way his voice sounded, his oos and rrrs and the ghs; the 's' words like suster, skaam, saggies, skitter. Funny that she can remember some of the words, but can't remember his name.

He was the one that had the fever so badly, she was sure he'd be dead by day-break. He kept calling out a name, a woman's name. One afternoon, when he could first sit again, he had motioned for his jacket, pulled a dog-eared photo from the inside breast pocket;

'My vrou.'

'Shall I write to her for you?' But he'd waved her gesturing hands away.

'Ek sal dit self doen.'

The next time death came calling, there was nothing Isabella, nor anyone else, could do for him. They heard the low thrum of the lions, where they sat, the men around the evening fire, Isabella in the shadow of her tent, head wrapped in fine netting, a small bunch of fragrant green twigs smouldering near her feet to ward off the mosquitoes. Where had he gone? Just to walk. He loved to walk out in the veld. Be careful, Old Solomon would caution, as he set off alone.

They had heard the lions, and Old Solomon had come from the labourer's camp with his kierie, her father had taken his gun from beneath his cot, and with some of the others, gone out, their torches far away stars in the dark, to look for him.

'*Tschwa*!! *Tschwa*!!' they had shouted at the lions, and a rifle shot cracked across the veld. And another. Then back they'd come, faces folded in on themselves.

It was Old Solomon, hat in hand, grey hair ribbed across his head, who brought one of the man's boots and the sleeve of a blood-soaked shirt to her father the next morning.

'Vir sy vrou,' said Old Solomon. 'Something to bury, so that his spirit can find its way home.'

Home. There is that word again. Isabella eases Ian's limp body out of her numbed arm and lays his head on her lap, the knitted frog in his hand. So like Ruthie to have made that frog, she thinks, looking at the dozing woman, and then at the Goldbergs, clutching each other, even in sleep, as if scared of being torn apart. The sky outside the train window is almost black now, except for the powdery moon-light sifting like fine flour into a bowl.

Isabella fingers her mother's silver bar-pin brooch with its little moon-shaped pearl pinned at the neck of her high collared shirt. She would hate to sell it. No, she would never sell it, her wedding band neither. She would rather nurse again if she had to, though George wouldn't care for it, now the war was over. Isabella doesn't want to think about what desperate times might mean for them in Johannesburg. She will not, no cannot, imagine what they will do if there's no house, no work, no food. If George's illness flares up again. Her brain simply stalls.

There would be the house – there had to be the house.

Isabella can see number nine standing there expectantly. For it seems suddenly to her that the house is longing for her return. Perhaps George is inside right at this moment, getting things to order, getting ready for them, knowing they are to arrive a mere fortnight after his own return on the first repatriation train.

No. Most likely not. Most likely he has taken lodgings somewhere. Most likely the wooden railings, the front door with its little glass panes and brass knocker, the floorboards, all their furniture, are now broken up, used as fire wood. The last winter had been desperately cold everywhere. Or perhaps a Boer family had taken advantage of the situation and moved in? There had already been one or two of them in the neighbourhood when they'd had to leave. Maybe not even a family, but a bunch of ruffians who stayed on to work the mines? Had deserters or commandos sheltered there? Their house would be gutted. Johannesburg had become a place of lawlessness. That's what the *Dispatch* said.

Irritated with herself, Isabella tries to reel in her imagination. George would have found them a place to stay even if number nine was no longer habitable. He would have found work. If the city needed rebuilding, they would need architects, wouldn't they? If not, what else? The Kirk? More charity? God forbid.

The train lurches, slows to a halt, wheels screeching. 'What is it?' says Mrs Harris, waking.

'Doesn't seem to be a station.' Mr Goldberg is peering out the window.

'Not the Boers,' wails Mrs Goldberg. 'Please God.'

'Sssh, be quiet.'

Ian sits bolt upright. 'Not to worry, my laddie, just watering the horses.' Isabella hugs him to her. It is what George would have said to him, just watering the horses.

Ian makes little snuffling noises, draws his knees up to his chest as if wishing to make himself smaller. 'I want Father.'

The baby begins to cry and Mrs Morgan hurries to nurse

him. Isabella can only see the top of the woman's head as she bends low over her baby, a dark bun of braided hair neatly coiled and pinned in typical Boer style. Perhaps she'll speak up for us?

From outside, the sound of feet, and then men's voices, coming closer. English voices. The guard jumps down from his van and goes towards them.

'It's only a checkpoint,' says Mr Goldberg. 'We must be nearing Burgersdorp?'

Isabella looks across at Mrs Morgan, and seeing her rigid, reaches over the aisle and pats her arm. The train begins to move.

'Not to worry,' she whispers. 'Not to worry. Just watering the horses.'

And now they can see the dark shapes of soldiers turning away from the train, others hunched around a small fire, a face lit up here and there, the ghostly white of a tent. Over there, in the distance, the glare of something much larger going up in flames, spitting sparks at the moon.

★

Mrs Hester Morgan is on her feet, staring out of Isabella's window. The railway line does not go past Bakenkop, Hester knows that, but had it gone just a few miles further east, it might have been her home they see burning, the glow of it growing smaller and smaller as they gather speed. The train jolts, and she lands clumsily next to Isabella.

'Ekskuus,' she says blankly.

'Here, take the window seat,' Isabella whispers. 'I'll hold your baby.'

Hester doesn't hesitate, thrusts him at Isabella and presses herself to the window. That would be the Jouberts' place, wouldn't it? But perhaps she is already losing her bearings. If only the moon were brighter, if only she could be sure. Is that Klaarfonteinkoppie? Or maybe Rooikop? Sometimes she and

Albertus would ride to the top of the Rooikop to see the train from Queenstown passing far away in the distance, on its way to Burgersdorp and Bloemfontein.

Liewe Vader, and where is Tannie Helene then? Do the English have her? And if it wasn't Rietfontein, then whose farm was it? The Venters'? The LeGranges'? How long since they'd past Molteno? Hester looks for the Southern Cross, but can't find it. Perhaps it is later than she thinks, perhaps they have long since passed every place she knows? But those koppies, they look so familiar.

I'm leaving, Hester thinks, I'm leaving this behind. Leaving the vlaktes, the veld and the koppies. Leaving home, leaving Bakenkop, with its proud white-washed house. Leaving the gardens, the outbuildings, barn and kraal standing so neatly in the werf, with no more than a low rock wall to hold back the bitterbos, the bloubos, the khaki veld and the Rooinekke. Was her Aia still there, still sweeping the stoep every morning with her besembos broom, *tssk tssk tssk*. Or was it all burnt?

Hester wants to scream, to howl, to fling herself from the train. To throw off the ridiculous black bonnet, hitch up her long black skirts, steal a horse and ride back home. For though she knew, when she married Reverend Graham Morgan, that Pa would never let her return, she still thinks of Bakenkop as home. She wants to shout, I'm sorry. I was wrong! But there is nobody there any more. Nobody to take her back. Nobody to forgive her.

Hester leans her forehead against the cold glass. There is nobody left. She wipes her nose on her sleeve, then turns from the window. She reaches towards Isabella, asking with her arms for the baby. He is still asleep, so is the boy with his head on the lavender blue of his mother's lap. So too the other children, and the grown-ups opposite. The whole carriage is silent. Only the train is awake, and the woman sitting next to her.

'What is your baby's name?' Isabella asks.

'Albert.'

Hester takes two pieces of dried peach from her pocket, and hands one to Isabella. The other she places carefully into her mouth. It tastes of orange sunshine, of summer-time at Bakenskop, and the sweet konfyt Ma used to make when Hester was a girl. *If she were alive, would Ma have forgiven me?*

'Thank you,' says Isabella. 'I don't know when last I ate a piece of fruit, or anything so sweet. That tasted like – well like sunshine, or honey.'

Hester nods. They sit quietly, side by side.

'Have you family in Johannesburg, Mrs Morgan?'

'No.' Then, 'Yes. My husband, he has family there.' Hester turns back to the window.

She's heard nothing from her own family. Not a word from Pa since she married. And only a note from Hendrik, shortly after the war started.

Pa is leaving the farm in Outa Bokkies' hands, what else can he do?

He has called the commando together. I am riding with them.

Hester and Graham had to leave the mission-station, it was not safe to stay. The Church insisted. But Hester hated Queenstown. Hated staying in Reverend Peters' parish bungalow. Hated being hemmed in by the Town Guard, by hostile eyes, at church, at the shops, along the main road. The women were the worst. She could almost hear their whisper, sssssspy, felt it stirred into the weak tea she suffered after every Sunday service.

Every day Graham scanned the notices pinned up in the square, or he'd find some reason, as a priest, to be about when any Boer prisoners were brought in. But they could not find news of her family. 'We have to trust in God,' Graham would say, 'God knows we cannot trust man in times like these.'

'... And also my brother's wife, though I don't know how to find her,' says Hester slowly, the idea claiming itself as such, though she hardly knows she's been thinking it. 'Albertus, that's my brother, my late brother, his wife wrote to us from Johannesburg. But it was a long time ago.'

Albertus. Why, that's the name of the man with the terrible fever, thinks Isabella.

'One day a parcel came from Johannesburg. Pa fetched it from Burgersdorp when he went for supplies. In the parcel were some of Albertus's clothes. And a note. It was signed by a Mrs Nelia Roos. We didn't even know he was married.'

'That is who you named your boy after, your late brother Albertus?'

'Yes.' There is a long pause. 'And for your King. It was my husband's idea. For Boer and for Brit, he said. He hated the war. But he died, of pneumonia, as you know, before it ended.'

'There is nothing for you here any more,' the Reverend Peters had said to Hester one afternoon when she carried the tea tray into his study. It was just before evensong, but he wasn't at his desk, he was in the arm chair near the window, with the morning's paper open on his lap. 'They are building a camp in East London for Boer women and children ... it's in the *Dispatch*.' He doesn't tell her what else the newspaper says. Farm burning is old news.

Hester puts the tea tray down on the little side table, careful not to rattle the bone china nor spill on the lacy tray-cloth. She doesn't tell him she read the paper before bringing it to him this morning with his post. She just stands back a little, so she doesn't have to watch his heavy jaw at work, pushing words out like sausages.

Reverend Peters wonders if she's heated the pot properly, can't abide his tea lukewarm, nor stewed, for that matter. He doesn't tell her that he's galled by the plans for the new camp, wooden houses with proper corrugated-iron roofs, a school, hospital and a store. Why, it was to be far better equipped than the tented refugee camp for her Majesty's own subjects right here in Queenstown, ever was. Still, he doesn't wish it on her.

She is Morgan's widow and the child is half English, after all. 'I think it would be best if you went to your in-laws. They will be able to look after you.'

Reverend Peters doesn't want to be responsible for her. He couldn't stand her Boer ways, so out of place in an Anglican parish, from the first. And besides, people will talk, are already talking, if the verger is to be believed.

'You won't have another chance once the refugees have gone.'

Reverend Peters has written to Reverend Morgan's brother in Johannesburg himself, taken the reply to the Mayor, argued her case. The Mayor is a member of his congregation, a reasonable man. Yes, he would ensure that a Mrs G. Morgan and infant were on the repatriation list.

'Your husband would want you to go to his family under the circumstances, for the child's sake, if nothing else. I can't keep you here much longer.'

A week later Reverend Peters gave her half a pound (from the collection plate) and a food parcel from the Relief Committee, same as everyone else. He warns her not to speak, at all, if she can help it.

'Mr Clifford Morgan will be waiting for you at Park Station' he said.

'Johannesburg's is not such a big place,' says Isabella, 'bigger than Queenstown, mind you. And you'll have to be very careful of course, but I'm sure you'll find her, your brother's wife.'

★

'Isabella dear, I hardly know how to say goodbye. You've been a good friend, a daughter to us, hasn't she, Mr Goldberg? To think what we have been through together these last years. And it is true what you said, everyone suffers when men fight.' Mrs Goldberg is crying and clutching onto Ian. He struggles to free himself from her stiff bosom. 'Good-bye my dear boy.

Don't you go giving your mother any trouble now, you hear? And listen to your father.' She gives him a little shake and lets him go.

'We're not quite there yet,' says Mr Goldberg, 'still plenty of time to say goodbye.'

Isabella writes her address on two slips of paper torn from the long-empty sandwich wrappings. 'Take this, Ruthie,' she says, giving her one 'and if for some reason we're not there, ask for us at St Mark's Church on Cavendish St. I've written that down too. Yeoville is not so very far from Doornfontein.'

'We're nearly there girls, we're nearly there. Look out for Papa,' says Mrs Harris. 'You can smell we're nearly there … it's the dust, isn't it? Never thought I'd be so pleased to smell it again.'

Isabella turns to Hester, leans over little Albert and hugs her. 'Here is my address, Mrs Morgan. Once you've had a chance to settle in, do come to see me. Or ask for us at St Mark's Church. They should know where to find us, if – if we've had to settle somewhere else. And if ever you should need help, or a place to stay, you won't hesitate, will you?'

Hester keeps a tight grip on her hand, 'Please, call me Hester,' she whispers.

It is late in the afternoon when the train finally pulls into Park Halt Station. The platform is crowded, but there is no band, no ceremony, just people looking for family. Beggars and thieves too no-doubt, thinks Isabella, keeping a tight hold on Ian with one hand and on her carpet bag with the other. And soldiers. Hester stands half behind her, not moving. Oh, where is George?

A man in ill-fitting clothes and a slouch hat sidles up, 'Need a place to stay Ma'am? A carriage maybe?'

'No thank-you,' says Isabella. 'My husband will be along any minute to collect us.'

'Perhaps, Ma'am, it would be best if you wait at the station master's office. There are ruffians about, ready to take advantage,

Ma'am, if you know what I mean. Crowd's thinning quickly.'

Isabella inclines her head. She turns to Mrs Morgan. 'Perhaps we should do as he suggests. It would be a sensible place for your brother-in-law to meet you,' Isabella says. 'Have you any way of knowing him?'

There is Mr C. Morgan, waiting just a few yards away. Even Isabella recognises him, he has the look of Reverend Morgan about him, only sterner. Hester sucks in her breath, then walks towards him. They say something to each other, Isabella can't hear what. Hester looks back and Mr C. Morgan lifts his hat, bows towards Isabella ever so slightly, then turns and walks away. Hester follows him off the platform.

'Well, well, well, and what do we have here?' and there is George, swinging Ian into the air, a close embrace for Isabella. 'My very own family come home.'

'It is a remarkable story, my dear,' George says as they walk towards Yeoville. "The street is a mess, a dreadful mess. Everything at sixes and sevens. But our house is quite safe. A bit worse for wear, and covered in that chalky dust you used to fuss about so much, but quite safe. The Kirk too.'

It is not as much of a hill as Isabella remembers, but the road is deeply rutted, and Ian is tired. George swings him up onto his shoulders. 'We'd better hurry, before it gets any darker.'

'Do be careful of yourself, George,' Isabella says. 'He's heavy.'

George is looking wan and wheezes terribly. 'I'm sorry,' he says, stopping to rest again, 'that we couldn't have a carriage. They're asking a small fortune for the shortest of distances.'

Here and there a lamp burns inside a window, the house around it still standing. They pass a plot full of rubble, run wild with weed, and another with a broken chimney where a house once stood. An incomplete wall riddled with bullet holes, more rubble. They turn into Honey Street. The house at number four is still standing, so is number six.

'Boers,' said George. 'I've not met them, but Mrs Roos

told me. Probably having to lie low for a bit. Mrs Roos is our neighbour, a widow. Moved in next door and runs it as a boarding house. Decent place. I've been taking my meals there.'

Number five is where the Munros should be, but it's empty and the windows are all splintered. Number eight is in a state too, and then ... across the road, number nine.

Isabella stops. It is her very own house. There are the three steps, the stoep. There is her front door. Isabella's legs don't seem to know whether to walk on or give way. George looks anxiously at her.

'I'm all right, George. It is just my legs are all excited.' They stand there together, looking, Ian between them. 'Our house is safe, and all our things, you say?'

'Mrs Roos took care of it. How she knew it was our house I don't know, perhaps someone came looking for you? But she did tell me that once she learned it was Sister Isabella's home standing empty next door, she did everything she could to keep it safe for you. She said something quite lovely ... how exactly did she put it? Ah, yes – "When you extend kindness, it always comes back to you." You nursed her husband, she said, years ago, in the Lowveld, Black-water fever, I think it was. He told her about you in the last letter he ever sent her. Poor chap was killed not long after that – by a lion.'

Isabella climbs the steps onto her front stoep and opens the door. Life can take us away from where we belong, but we don't lose the longing for it, she thinks. If we are lucky we get to make our way back. And find it is still there.

Could Be

'We don't mean to say to people they can't walk around at 3 a.m.,' Western Cape Social Development MEC, Albert Fritz continued, 'but these are very different and difficult times. Please ensure that you don't place yourself in danger. That you are safe and go with people you can trust, who won't hurt you.'

– *Cape Times* 8 February 2013

There it is again. The thin tap of a branch against the bedroom window, though there had been no hint of a wind when she went to bed, nothing to stir the sea, flat as a lake, nor the candle-like cypresses that guard the garden path. And then something louder, something startling, and now she is awake. Toby is barking.

'In this year alone, we have seen incidents that have left us shaken.' The *Sunday Independent* lies open across her chest. In her hand reading glasses. Rainbow-framed. What was it that left us shaken? Something somebody had said? Liz pulls herself up from the cramp she'd slumped into. Tips the newspaper on the floor. No, it was the girl in Bredasdorp. Raped. Mutilated. Murdered.

Outside, a car stops, a door slams. She hears a man's voice. 'Ciao. Bye. Thanks hey.' Hears noisy male merriment in reply, but can't decipher the words. A big engine revs. There's rubber on the salt wind coming through the open window. Toby barks again, this time from right on the street. Damn it, she thinks, he's got out.

'Here boy, come on, come to me, there's a good dog.'

Now the man's voice is calling her dog, well Peter's dog actually. Liz swings her legs out of the narrow bed, and hooks back the curtain. The bougainvillea, thick with flowers, papery now and colourless in the dim street light, shrouds her view of the road. She remembers the council men in their orange overalls, putting up the metal guard around the front of the globe so that the bright light wouldn't disturb her childhood sleep, but fall instead, more usefully, around the base of the pole, on the pavement, now overgrown with weeds and mined with dog turd.

'Water and lights still take precedence over the safety of women & children.' That's what people are taking action about, shaken or not. How insufficient the country's outrage.

Liz would call out to Toby, but she doesn't want to wake her mother sleeping in the next room. She will have to go out if she wants to get him. She listens for the man's voice again. All quiet now. She counts to one hundred. Still quiet. All right then.

At the bottom of the passage, Liz deactivates the alarm, unlocks the door, crosses the lounge, unlocks the front door, then the security gate, and steps outside. It is Sunday, the 10th of February, 2013. It is a suburb of Cape Town, South Africa. Rape Capital of the World. She should know better. Liz sees tomorrow's headline: **Woman Should Have Known Better.**

There is a light wind, a breeze too warm for a South Easter. A Berg wind, maybe? Liz walks down the path, unlocks and opens the garden gate. The tarred pavement is crinkly under her adult feet, the moon insignificant overhead. 'Toby,' she calls, 'Toby?'

'Is he yours? The black dog?'

Liz jerks round, another headline forming ... **One in Three**

South African Women. It's the voice she heard from inside. The voice calling 'goodbye', calling, 'here boy'. She sees he is young, younger than his voice, but swarthy and heavyset. Sees the dark, matted hair, a forehead filmed in sweat, and takes a careful step backwards, towards her front gate. **Woman Attacked Outside Mother's House.**

The street is completely empty, dark spaces pool between each street light. Not a car passes. There is a rip where the arm of his white T-shirt joins at the shoulder.

'Yes,' she says, and tries to whistle for Toby, turning away, then flicking back again, not wanting to give him opportunity to surprise her, to catch her unaware. She tries whistling again. Where is that damn dog? 'Toby, Toby,' she calls, and again 'T-o-b-e-e-e' louder now, wanting to create a disturbance, wake a neighbour.

'Ran off that way.'

Liz half looks the way he points, but keeps him squarely in her sights.

'Does he know his way around here?'

'No.'

'We better look for him then. Could get lost, or run over. We can take my car.'

Liz notices the we. Notices he sounds concerned, not drunk, not aggressive.

'It's parked just over there.' He indicates up the road. 'I live two doors up.'

Liz thinks of telling him, No thanks ... I'll just go back inside. She thinks, I'm not risking my life for a dog. She thinks of phoning Peter in the morning ... 'Your bloody stupid dog escaped the garden and ran off. No, not back yet.' He would never expect her to go looking for Toby, not in the middle of the night. But how can she just abandon Toby? Not even she could do that to a dog.

Liz thinks of the Yale-lock snapping closed behind her on the garden gate, of the short distance between it and the security gate. She sees herself turning the lock on the front door, turning the key in the passage door, re-activating the alarm, walking back down the passage, and listening for Toby (and the man) from her bed.

She hears voices in her head saying, 'Of course you should go back inside! That's the only sensible thing to do.' She sees the faces of those who have always cautioned her: there are her late father and her mother, her older siblings Lauri and Adam. There is Peter. There is her ex-husband Michael and there is Rupert, their son, and Stella, not daddy's little girl any more. There are her walking friends, Jo, Olivia, Paula and Margie, shaking their heads at her, 'Be careful,' they say, 'don't do anything stupid.' There are Trixi and Pat, who trained her as a volunteer counsellor at Rape Crisis. There is the crowd of women with whom she has marched, over and over again. 'Enough is Enough,' they are saying. 'Take Back the Night.' It is they who are saying, 'Mr Fritz, those who are raped do not "place themselves" in danger; it's the rapists who place them in danger.'

'That's kind of you to offer,' she says, 'but no thanks.' There is no pause then, no hesitation. Her sentence slides on through the full stop straight into ... 'We'll go in my car. Just give me a moment to get my keys.' Liz is surprised not to be surprised at herself. She walks back along the garden path and into the house, no backward glance, down the passage and into her bedroom. This is crazy, she thinks. **Woman Makes Big Mistake.** Her car keys are where they are supposed to be: Top left hand drawer. Surely that's a good sign?

On her way out again, Liz pauses at her mother's bedroom door. Her breathing is the slow, untroubled breathing of the heavily sedated, no chance she'll wake up till morning.

Outside the man is waiting beside her car. He has a leash in one hand, dog biscuits in the other. **Victim Tied Up With Dog Leash.** Liz unlocks the car, and climbs in. The man climbs in the front seat and slams the door.

'I'm a bit of a dog-man,' he says, 'have three of them myself, Pointers. I couldn't live with myself if anything happened to them.'

In her small car, Liz can taste the whiskey on his breath, the closed-up-room smell of him, and something else ... something cloying ... sweet, like fabric softener? The doors lock automatically when she starts the engine. Woman Locked in Car with Criminal.

'I haven't got into a car with a strange man since I gave up hitch-hiking ...' Liz stops herself saying in the 80s, not wanting to give away her age in case it makes her seem, ... frail? 'Which way did you see him go?' She tries for confident, commanding, strong.

'Up The Fairways, I think I saw him headed that direction. I'm Charles, by the way.' He winds down the window. 'Sorry, I must stink a bit. Been out with some friends.'

Liz swings her car right, into the road which curves past the darkness of the Little Glen. A few lights flicker through the wind-worried leaves from the flats across the green space. On her side of the road the houses are dark, except for perimeter lighting.

The clock on the dash says 3 a.m.

They drive past the house where Tammy and her disgusting brother Murray used to live. Past where Alison and her nearly-as-disgusting brother David used to live (where Liz once threw up at a sleep-over from scoffing too many sweets, and was never invited back), past Victor's (who was caught stealing from the school tuck-shop in standard six) and the whatcha-ma-call-its ... Daniel and Jason ... the Greenbergs. She used to know who lived in almost every house along this street, could've leaned out her window and called for help by name. Woman Kidnapped in Childhood Neighbourhood.

Liz drives around the block, slows when they come level with the house Charles indicated earlier. That other smell about him? Dagga. Of course. The boy who sat next to her in maths everyday after long break, smelt just like that.

'Go again.'

Drug Addict Forces Woman to Drive in Circles All Night.

'Okay, let's try Victoria Road, now. Maybe he's gone down to the beach,' Charles says.

They drive along Victoria Road at 30 km/h. Charles watches out his window. Liz watches Charles out the corner of her eye. They pass palm tree after palm tree, no dog. **Woman Smashes Car into Tree to Disarm Captor.**

Charles's hair is curly, where he's run his fingers through it. More curly than matted, and yes dark, very dark, almost black, and overgrown. His right ear and the top part of his jaw are hidden in the curls, but she can see a scratch of beard climbing up his neck to a full top lip. She licks her own lips again, feels the thinness of them, wonders how long until they adopt that permanently bereft look her mother's mouth has. Her own hair is straight, well cut, and defiantly grey. She tries mushing it up a little, to lift the bits flattened by sleep, push them into shape. Liz leans out the window and manages a whistle.

'See anything?'

'Uh uh. Nothing. No Toby.'

'Make a U-turn then,' he says. 'Pull over.'

The multi-coloured fairy lights strung between the palm trees have long been removed. Each tree stands in a circle of sandstone paving with port-hole style spotlights beneath them. The old street lights are still there, still light the pavement and the usually full parking bays, but the grass down to the beach is dark. The beach even darker. There is no-one around. This is it, Liz thinks, the site of the crime. She can almost see the red and white tape cordoning off the scene, and curses her stupidity, her stubbornness, her sense of entitlement. **Woman's Solo 'Take Back the Streets' Campaign Meets Bloody End.**

'I'm going to check the beach. Try up past Glen Beach, then

meet me back here. Okay?' Charles jumps out, walks around to her side of the car, puts his head in the window, his hands gripping the window sill. He has big hands, exceptionally long fingers. They could choke the life out of anyone. 'We'll find him,' he says. 'Don't look so worried.'

Liz watches his dark head cross the lawn, drop down towards the sand and disappear. This is her moment to escape. This is an opportunity to be sensible. She will drive off now, hide the car in her mother's double garage, walk back inside, and lock all the doors. That would be that. **Woman Has Narrow Escape.**

Liz drives back along the beach front, up the hill towards Glen Beach. No dog. She drives past the bowling green. No dog. She turns around at the end of Fourth Beach (still no damn dog) and heads back. She hesitates at the bottom of Strathmore Road, direct route to her mother's house, but keeps to Victoria Road, to the rendezvous point. It's only fair, he's been so helpful really. It would be rude to simply drive off, to abandon him when he's being so kind. **Good Manners the Death of Her.**

Charles isn't there. Liz stares at the spot empty of Charles. This is the place he'd said? Right? Dumped. Never mind driving off, she's been dumped.

No, there he is, coming this way. Liz climbs out of the car and walks onto the grass.

'No luck?'

'No luck,' she says.

'Me neither. But the water is unbelievably warm. Want a swim?

'Okay. Sure. Why not?' **Woman in Deep Water.**

The sand is cold, but he's right, the water is warm and the waves are small, more a peaking and a subsidence than actual waves.

Charles pulls his shirt over his head. 'Look,' he says, 'over there ... phosphorescence.'

Liz follows the line from his finger out to sea and back again, up his arm, across his shoulder, down his chest. She looks away when he drops his jeans, steps out of his boxers.

'Ready?'

'You go in, I'll come in a while.'

Liz is not in a mini skirt. Liz is not wearing high-heels, but she has nothing on under her draw-string pyjama pants. Her belly, once flat as an ironing board, pouts a little, her pubic hair, once thick and tight as wet moss, is now sparse. Her breasts look despondent, unable to face the world eye-to-eye without an underwire bra. Still she has a good body, a certain sexiness, she knows she does, regardless of being unable to stir Peter (or herself) to action as often as she used to.

Liz wades into the sea, letting her fingers trail lightly across the surface. She is taken by a wash of feeling, a swelling that begins in her pelvis, lifts her from her feet and makes her weightless. She feels her nipples bristle, and rolls onto her back, floating feet first over the waves, feels the suck and swell of salt water. She tilts her head back and lets her ears fill, listens like a whale to the groans and moans of the ocean-body. She imagines herself a buoyant sea creature free from the crushing weight of gravity, of her gender, her nationality, her age. She imagines not having to worry, for Stella, or herself, or her eighty-two-year-old mother, or any other woman.

Liz swims further out. Not old ladies' breaststroke, but the firm and confident backstroke she learnt at adult swim classes. She passes Charles who is treading water, and keeps going, concentrating on her strokes. But the Milky Way soon blurs with salt water and Liz is swamped by a wave of sadness. That is not how the world is. It doesn't matter what she does, or what she doesn't do. It doesn't matter how careful, how sensible, how foolish she is. The odds are against her. Against Stella. Against her eighty-two-year-old mother. There are three of them. One will be hurt. Badly hurt. Most likely killed, and not kindly either. Liz's nose and mouth fill with brine. She thinks she will drown half way out to Whale Rock, escaping an act of kindness.

Liz is exhausted by the time her toes touch sand again. She wades towards shore and onto the beach. Charles is standing there, already in his jeans.

'Jesus,' he says, 'I didn't think you were a crazy woman.' He rubs her back with his shirt. Rough, clumsy swipes. Liz can't keep her teeth from chattering. He wraps his shirt around her. 'You okay?'

Liz wants his arms, not his shirt. Wants to push her luck. There are no statistics for kindness, no prevalence ratings. No awards. **Cape Town: Kindness Capital of the World.**

'You'd better get dressed,' he says, stooping to pick up her clothes and handing them to her. 'Warm up a bit and then we can go find that dog of yours.'

Liz follows him back to the car. He takes her hand when they reach the steps. She feels elated, grateful. For assistance up uneven stairs in the dark? No. What does it matter what Peter would say? What Trixie or Pat would think? How her mother or the children will remonstrate with her? What does it matter that she is hand-in-hand with a stranger, who is helping her up the steps from the beach onto the damp lawn, across the newly paved path and to her car at 3.30 a.m. in the morning? What does it matter if he is thinking of his girlfriend now, has tired of helping a middle-aged woman look for her dog and wants to get home? She is alive. She has got into a car with a total stranger. She has driven dark streets with someone she took for a dope-smoking drunk. She has swum out further than she has ever swum in her life, day or night. She has felt the suck and swell of sea. Felt the undertow. She has ignored common sense, ignored women's fate. She has taken a stupid risk, all for a stupid dog (a dog, for God's sake!), but she has defied the odds. She is unharmed, un-mutilated ... alive. This is not how the world is, but it could be.

'Let's go up Berkley Road and see if we find him heading home,' Charles says.

Liz starts the car, slides into first gear and eases her foot off the clutch. They do not open their windows. Liz wonders if his dope buzz is close enough to have made her high too. She feels intoxicated. At the top of Berkley, just before she swings into Sedgemoor Road, they see the dog, tongue out, panting, just a few hundred metres from her front gate.

'Must've been some bitch on heat right around here,' Charles says.

Liz pulls over and Charles opens his door. Toby climbs straight in, settles himself at Charles' feet, tail thumping.

'Toby! Where have you been, stupid dog?' Liz says.

Toby ignores her.

'You had us worried old boy,' Charles says. Toby licks Charles' hands, puts his front paws on his knee and licks his face. He eats the biscuits Charles brought for him, crumbs dropping between the seats.

Liz parks beneath the syringa tree, waits for the two of them to stop kissing and cuddling. 'Right then,' she says, still grinning. 'Thank you very much, Dog-Man.'

She holds onto Toby's collar while Charles walks up to his house.

Liz waits until 7 p.m. the next evening. She has given her mother supper and made her comfortable. Liz wants to return the blue lead she found left in her car, and to say thank you properly to Charles, give him a bottle of Johnny Walker.

She stands outside the front door two houses up and rings the bell. A much older man, a man roughly her own age, answers the door. Liz asks for Charles. It takes her a little while to understand: nobody called Charles lives there. Liz steps back to check the number next to the front door.

'This is number 18a?' she says. 'What about 18b?'

The man says two women live next door, but that they are away at the moment. He has the keys to their house in case of emergencies, and is clearing the *Cape Times* from their post box everyday while they are gone.

'No, they don't have a house-sitter. No dogs either,' he says.

'What about across the road?' Perhaps Charles meant two doors up on the other side of the street. But the man doesn't know who drives the white BMW or the black Mini Cooper S parked there, doesn't know who lives opposite his front door, or up the street. He only knows this one set of neighbours.

'Good luck,' he says as he closes the door. At least that's what it sounds like.

Liz crosses the road and pushes the buzzer on the intercom beneath a big brass number 15. A woman answers.

'Yes? Who? Sorry.'

At the next house, it's the same story – and the next, and the next. Now she is four houses up and has tried both sides of the street.

There is no Charles.

Liz leans down and pats Toby's head. 'Don't look so worried,' she says. 'We'll find him.'

What It Takes

In the corner is an old cast iron stove. J & C.G. Bolinders of Stockholm. Four plates; an oven with three doors. On the largest, two words: Stango, and Open. Beneath, a smaller, oblong door, labeled Soot Door. The third door is much the same, but without the writing. Each door has a different pattern intricately moulded into the black iron, and a coiled, silver wire handle. There is a rail along one side of the stove on which to hang oven gloves or dishcloths.

Polla used to warm Edvard's socks along a rail like that in the dark mornings, while his coffee was brewing and his pap cooking. She used to keep a fire going in the old stove all winter, leave a pot of stew, or mutton curry simmering for days. Standing there in the Sutherland Museum, Evelyn can almost hear the rasp of heavy pots drawn along its surface, the rattle of the stoker Polla used to poke the fire.

It is summer on the farm. The big black stove is redundant. Polla is frying Edvard's lunch on the gas stove, lamb chops in one pan, chips in another. She is muttering under her breath because the gas stove is temperamental, doesn't heat nice and even like the Bolinders. The chops are not cooking to her liking. The last of the fresh carrots have been grated and mixed with tinned pineapple to make a salad. A bottle of Ma's beetroot and a tin of baked beans are on the Formica topped kitchen table waiting to be decanted into serving bowls.

(Or had she given up caring by then? Perhaps she had already told Polla not to bother with salads, serving bowls and decanting things?)

Now Edvard's diesel bakkie is coming along the road. Evelyn hears him pull up under the quince tree outside the kitchen door. She hears the crunch of his boots on the gravel, the screen door's hinge as it stretches open, and the thud of it as it whacks back into the door frame.

If he is in a good mood, he might tell her to pour him some Coke and be sure to put lots of ice in it. Then he might say, what a kak day it was so far, forget the ice, fill it up with some Klippies. Or he might say he's changed his mind, he wants a Castle, and it better be really cold.

And then, there's another kind of mood where he might tell her to go change her clothes ... he doesn't like the way she has her shirt tied under her tits, like a hoer. Or to put some make-up on, she looks like shit. Not a good mood, but not a bad one either.

In a bad mood, chops and chips would be on the floor. Glass jar and bowls shattered. Beetroot red on the wall.

Evelyn can't tell if the smell of burning is coming from somewhere in the museum, or if she is imagining it. She turns from the kitchen implements, walks past the other displays and out through the door. She walks along Jubilee Street, back to the restaurant in Voortrekker Road, where Kate's waiting for her.

'Anything interesting?' Kate asks, pulling her reading glasses off her nose so she can see Evelyn in focus.

'Not much. Mostly old farm tools and kitchenware. That kind of thing.'

Kate hadn't wanted to go to the museum. 'I'll wait for you at the restaurant' she'd said. 'I'll order for you.' She said she'd hate to see what they've done with the fossil display. Besides, it is her policy not to have anything to do with hominids specifically, and museums in general, when she is on holiday. It is a glorious winter day, the kind only the Karoo can dish up.

The usual assortment of shops and small town buildings line Voortrekker Road, some Victorian, built with sandstone, some concrete uglies. It is election month. Every lamp post sports a poster: COPE. SACP – for Madiba. DA. ANC. An elderly couple in matching tracksuit pants and yellow jerseys walk past the restaurant window holding hands. A man in blue overalls, pegged at the ankle, peddles by. The ubiquitous farmers' bakkies, Isuzus or Toyatas, are parked outside the bank, or the post office, or *FoodZone*. They're all the same dun colour from the dust. One or two fancier cars with CA registrations cruise past.

'We out of tomatoes. Sorry,' the proprietor says, plonking their toasted cheese sans the tomato, down on the table. She has lots of wavy brown hair, was probably pretty once. 'You lucky you wasn't here a week ago, it was minus two, and it's only May. This town doesn't only have the darkest skies, it also has the lowest temperatures in the country, you know.' She rattles the last part off as if she's reading from a travel brochure: *Interesting Facts about Sutherland*.

'Yes.' says Evelyn. 'I know. I'm from around here.'

'Really? Where from?'

'Fraserburg.'

'No way. I wouldn't have guessed it.'

Evelyn knows she's taking in her chic haircut, her perfectly made up face. Her Cape Storm jacket.

'Not much happening there, these days, or so I hear. Not that here's much better. Still, at least we have the telescopes and the tourism. And no crime, not like you ous in the cities.' She takes the salt, pepper and Old Gold tomato sauce from the neighbouring table, puts it down in front of them. 'All the young people is leaving. I should of gone too, when I had a chance. Not much for a person in these parts.' She swipes at a smear on the table with the corner of her apron. 'You visiting family?'

'Yes.' says Evelyn. She is thinking of the two little graves on the west kopjie, and the one in the Fraserburg Cemetery. Elsa Evelyn Ockers. 29 September 1981.

The waitress moves off, saying, 'Coffee's coming, hot milk or cold?' as she goes.

'I didn't know you still had family here,' says Kate.

★

The pain begins a few hours before dawn. Evelyn thinks her periods have started, it is the same long-fingered kind of pain clawing away at her abdomen. Then she remembers, no, it's been twenty four weeks and five days, to be exact, since she last had them.

But there is wet between her legs. Could it be her waters? She's read you can leak amniotic fluid – that it isn't so good for the baby, but not necessarily a crisis. Evelyn rolls onto her side and sits up on the edge of the bed. She lights the gas lamp, and goes down the passage to the toilet. A bright stain on her white cotton panties. That's worse isn't? She shouldn't bleed at this stage, not like this?

Evelyn thinks of phoning Ma. But the whole district would know about it if she calls anyone at four am. Mrs Nommer-Asseblief at the exchange will listen in and broadcast the news, sure as anything. Everyone would know that Evelyn Ockers had panicked at the sight of a little blood and thought she was going to lose her baby.

She will stay calm. Maybe the pain will go away, it seems to be dulling a little? Maybe the bleeding will stop? In the kitchen, Evelyn lights the stove and puts the kettle on. Not dulling. Sharpening. Like a bush-saw it pulls its teeth this way, then pushes them back that way. This way and that way.

She walks around the kitchen table, waiting for the water to boil, one hand at the small of her back, the other, a fist, pressed to her stomach.

When the pain subsides a little, she makes a cup of rooibos, sits on Polla's stool, and takes a few sips. When the pain begins again, she paces around the table, up the passage, back to the kitchen.

By the time the exchange opens, Evelyn has changed her pad three times and can hardly speak when the pain bites.

'Nommer asseblief?'

'9347 Tannie.' she says.

Ma tells her to get into the bakkie and drive towards Fraserburg. Does she think she can drive? Yes? Good. She must take Polla with her to open the gates. Polla is there, right? Ma will leave immediately. She will meet Evelyn along the way, Evelyn must just go slowly. Ma will call Dr Bruwer. Is she dressed? No? Well she should not bother about it now. Put a towel on the seat. She must set off straight away. She must drive carefully, and pull over when the pain is too bad. Ma is coming.

Evelyn sits in the bakkie until she sees Polla coming along the path towards the house, then starts the engine, reverses out from under the tree. Stalls. Jerks to a stop.

Polla is running. Polla is beside the bakkie. Polla is asking questions. She is looking at Evelyn slumped in the driver's seat. Polla is saying, 'Liewe Jesus. Liewe, liewe Jesus'.

The pain is strapped to her now. Strands of pain plait themselves tightly about her middle, like the tourniquet Pa used when the Cobra got him on the leg. Her breath is jagged. She cannot get enough air. It is as if the pain has pushed a throbbing lump up into her throat.

'Missus must breathe more slowly. Slowly. Slowly, Missie Evelyn,' says Polla in a sing-song voice. 'Slowly. Slowly, Missie Evelyn. Slowly.' Polla cannot drive, but she can sing.

Evelyn drives between contractions. Sixty-five kilometres of dirt road and nine farm gates separate Verlatenkloof from town. She drives twenty-eight kilometres, and Polla opens seven gates before they see the dust of Ma's car approaching. It is only ten to eight.

★

Edvard does not know about Elsa Evelyn Ockers, until a week after her funeral. He is on ops somewhere on the border. The army lets him home from South West on a special four-day pass.

Edvard is thinner than when Evelyn saw him last, and darker. His arms around her are harder. Meaner. He doesn't know to hold her gently because her breasts are still sore and leaking. He wants her to cry. He wants to know what went wrong. Was something wrong with it, or with her? Dr Bruwer comes to see him, to explain. It is no-one's fault. Dr Bruwer must have also told him no sex, because Edvard doesn't even try.

Edvard wants Evelyn to stay on at her Ma's in town. But Evelyn just wants to go back to Verlatenkloof. She wants to be left alone with the soft baby things in the new wooden chest of drawers in the second bedroom on the right, as you go down the passage. The room with the one curtain of pale blue she embroidered with white stars, already hung, just to see how it looks. The other curtain, still waiting for its stars, is folded in her sewing basket. She wants to sit in the rocking chair her mother sat in when she nursed Evelyn as a baby. She wants these things to tell her that her baby, her baby Elsa, was real.

And she wants to get far away from town, from the people who will keep coming to visit. She especially wants to get away from Liesl, Mariska and Annette, who insist it is no trouble to pop in after each exam, who can't resist describing their Matric Dance dresses, or discussing who is going with who. Maybe they will let you come to the dance now, they say.

'Edvard. Please. Take me back to the farm. Ma will agree to whatever you say.'

'If you want, but I won't be back for at least three or four months. They are sending us to Angola.'

On the third night, the night before he has to return to Rundu, Evelyn finds him in the baby's room, sitting in the rocking chair. Every drawer is open and baby things are strewn across the floor. The curtain has been pulled down and the arm ripped from the teddy-bear Edvard had bought soon after she had told him she was pregnant. There is an empty Klipdrift bottle on the floor.

Edvard is crying. Snot and tears running down his face. He doesn't look up at her. 'All for nothing hey, Evey? All this. It's a joke, hey? This baby stuff ... for nothing. Moving onto Verlatenkloof, getting married, turns out it's all for nothing. You could have got your Matric, Evey. You could've become an air hostess like you wanted.'

Evelyn stands behind him and rubs her hand gently over his shorn head, and then, when he doesn't shrug her off, crosses her arms across his chest, and buries her face in his neck.

'And do you know what? You not the only one who wanted to get out of here. I also wanted to do something with my life when I finally finish with the fucking army and before being landed on a fucking sheep farm just because it's what E.P. Ockers have been doing since the fucking trek-boers got here. Whose idea was all this anyway? Not mine, Evelyn. It wasn't my poes of an idea.'

★

Kate and Evelyn drive out of Sutherland, up past the observatory, down the other side, and onto the flat, stony vlaktes that glitter out to the horizons like silvery lakes, kilometre after kilometre.

'You can see this was all under the sea millions of years ago,' Kate says.

When they reach a crossroad, they stop to take a photo of the old fashioned sign post, black with pressed white lettering, like something out of a 1940's movie. One arm points east to Fraserburg, one west to Sutherland, the others north to Williston and south to Merweville. All of them at least an hour away. An old wind-pump stands scarecrow still, 'Lloyds Wynberg', still visible on its vane. Four of its blades are broken. The cement dam it once pumped for is empty. Except for silt.

'I'd forgotten how desolate it is here.' Evelyn says. She starts the car again, presses a little harder on the accelerator now. A dust trail stands to attention in a straight line behind them. The road is longer than she remembers. Fences still line it on both sides, with strips of plastic and straggly wisps of sheep's wool caught here and there on the barbs. Telephone wires dip between each telephone pole in a predictable rhythm.

They see an abandoned farm house, and stop again, this time for Kate to photograph the Victorian architecture, poke around the werf and visit the graveyard. They open the front gate, curly wrought iron, once painted white. The stoep is wooden, like the turned and peeling pillars holding up the curved corrugated iron roof. The strip of wooden brookie-lace hanging from the eave is broken in places, whole pieces of it fallen on the ground. The front door, flanked by two large sash windows, is locked. The windows are so dirty and scoured by sand, it is difficult to see through them. A lean-to barn has been added onto one side of the house. Inside, signs of fairly recent animal habitation, the earth floor covered with hoof-prints, old cow pats, sheep dung, and straw.

Through the barn, an open door leads into the house. Inside, high ceilings; a swallow's nest against the elaborate cornices. Walls painted cornflower blue, faded now; chunks of plaster missing. Two large front rooms. In one, a wooden crate up-ended. On it, a candle stub in a sardine tin, with a box of Lion matches tucked neatly alongside. An iron bedstead with a cardboard box split open and laid flat across the springs for a mattress. The floor has been swept clean.

'Shepherds?'

'Or karretjiemense maybe. They used to do most of the shearing out here.'

In the kitchen, a large hearth built into the wall still holds the ashes of a fire. A few floor boards are missing, and the shutters on the kitchen windows are hanging skew. Nothing moves. The kitchen door is open, the ground outside thick with weeds grown lanky in the shade. Outside a wooden staircase leads to the attic.

In the yard, Evelyn finds the opening to a well under a few planks. 'The new owners probably have another farm somewhere else, a bigger one, with a better house. They would have needed more water and grazing. Even when I was growing up, farmers were already struggling to make enough profit with the number of sheep only one farm can support.'

A little way away from the house is a grove of gnarled trees, and beneath them a graveyard, surrounded by the same wrought iron fencing as the gate to the house.

'The Marais family lived here,' Kate says. 'Look, here: François Hendrik Marais, died 1809. This has to be the oldest grave. And here, the latest one, Nikolaus Hendrik, born 1963, died 1964 ... only a year old. Oh, and a Helena Magdalene, just a few months old. The poor mother.'

'There were lots of them, the Marais ... it's one of the oldest families around here. These ones probably got rich during the wool boom judging by the house.'

'Verlatenkloof wasn't anything like this, was it?'

'I keep forgetting, you never really got to see it, did you? No, the house was nothing like this. Verlatenkloof's house was squat and ugly. Poky rooms stuffed full of his Ouma's old furniture, horrible ball and claw stuff. The windows were small because of the heat, but they rattled non-stop in the wind, and there were these horrible brown curtains. No, the house wasn't anything like this one. But the landscape, the veld – that's the same. Remember the twin kopjies, on the way to the house? There was a sort of ridge between them you had to drive over to get to us? I used to love those kopjies. I would climb up the west one, to see the sunset any chance I got.'

Evelyn is crying. Softly. Wipes her eyes on the edge of her sleeve.

'Evelyn?'

'Earlier. When I said about family, it was my babies, I was talking about. It wasn't just Elsa, Kate, there were two more. I never told you. Saskia and Dewald.' She says their names awkwardly, as if they are words from a foreign language. 'I miscarried twice more, at twelve weeks, I called the baby Saskia, and a year later, at fourteen weeks, a boy. Dewald.'

Kate puts her arms around her friend and holds her. 'Oh Eve. I'm so, so sorry.'

'I never told anyone about them. Not Edvard. Not Ma, she had already moved to Malmesbury by then. Not Polla. I buried them on the west kopjie, by myself. They were so little, Kate, so little, but almost perfectly formed already. I never got to see Elsa. With her it was so painful, so messy and strung out. By the time I reached the doctor, I was completely hysterical and he had to dope me up for the trip to Beaufort West, there wasn't a hospital in Fraserburg, then. They did a D&C under aesthetic and kept me more or less out of it for three days. But with the other two, it was different. With Saskia and with Dewald. They came so quickly, not so much pain. Edvard never knew. Nobody knows, except now you.'

'I'm sorry, Evelyn.' Kate can't think of anything more to say. She strokes Evelyn's hair. 'What you must have gone through, and so alone. And losing two more ... on top of everything else. I don't know how you coped.'

'I didn't cope. It nearly drove me mad. I think I might have gone mad, seriously insane, if you hadn't come when you did. If I hadn't seen you that one day, at the Caltex garage, of all places. I almost hadn't gone with Edvard, I hated going into town by then. I can't remember why I did. But if I hadn't ...'

★

The south wind pulls at her, unravelling her fragile composure. She would be fine if only they would leave her alone. If only the wind would drop. But they come at her in little dust-swirling eddies and in great roof-ripping gusts. At least she can see the south wind coming, the clouds first rallying along the skyline, then moving relentlessly towards her, the edge of a breeze lifting her skirt, a loose end of her hair brushing across her face, the laundry, stiff and lifeless, beginning to flap like khorhans preparing for take-off.

But unlike the wind, the women come without warning. Evelyn cannot see the tell-tale lines of dust over the dry veld on the other side of the twin kopjies which cut her and Edvard off from the rest of the world. There is nothing between their arrival and her first sighting, the flash of sun on a car roof, the low groan of an engine clearing the rise. There is no time to brush her hair, or change into a clean shirt. No time to hide.

Here they come. Mariska (now Mev Ds Joachim Moller), Annette (now Mev Ludewyk Rossouw, the butcher's wife) and Liesl (now Mev Kobus De Waal, whose husband farms the other side of town). Those same three girls from school. Girls who still live by the school motto, 'Daar is Werk'. Evelyn is their work now, their current project.

When Evelyn sees the car, she tells Polla to go home and not to come back until tomorrow. She loves old Polla, doesn't want to scandalise her. But she doesn't want her visitors to ever come back again either.

'Missus Evelyn mustn't be snaaks with the ladies,' Polla says on her way out. 'There is ginger beer in the fridge. And rusks in the tin.'

Evelyn waits on the stoep.

Liesl battles the driver's door open against the wind. Strains of 'Lady in Red' wander out of the car. Mariska and Annette get out on the other side, both of them covering their babies with a blanket to protect them from the dust. Out the back of the bakkie climbs one, two, three nannies, dressed in blue, lilac and pink overalls, with ruffled aprons and matching doeks. Each one has a toddler or two by the wrist and a big patchwork bag over their shoulders. The toddlers howl against the sand. It's in their faces, stinging their legs. The nannies pick them up, follow their madams across the yard and up the red-painted stairs, onto the sheltered stoep.

'Tjoe, but this wind is awful out here by you. How do you stand it Evelyn?'

The three laugh at its awfulness, as if the wind was something novel. They shake the sand from the baby blankets, dust it from the heads and shoulders of their children, run careful fingers through their own hair, giving little tosses of their heads to revive their Salton-Curler flicks.

Evelyn doesn't have flicks. Not even a fringe.

'Say hello to Tannie Evelyn,' Liesl tells the children. But the children press their faces into their nannies' necks and won't look.

Evelyn won't look at them either.

'Aren't you going to ask us in Evey?' Annette asks, 'Or are we going to kuier out here on the stoep in this bloody wind?'

Evelyn stands back from the front door. The three kiss her cheek as they pass, pressing their babies up against her as they do. Evelyn keeps her face slightly turned, so the kisses land near her ear. She sees the leaves on the old quince tree across the yard, vrommeled, from the heat or disease, she will have to ask Edvard. No, better not to.

She tries not to smell the softness of Elizabeth Anne Baby Shampoo, of Johnson and Johnson Baby Powder, of milk that has already turned to curd. Evelyn lets the screen door bang behind her, closes the front door, and follows her guests into the cramped sitting room, where the heavy brown curtains are closed against the heat.

The three women open the patchwork baby bags they made themselves, and pull out blankets for the children and nannies to sit on ('... to protect your carpet, you won't believe how much mess kids can make ... our rugs are ruined already'). One produces a box of Lego, another some wooden blocks and a few matchbox cars ('... we know you don't have any toys for them to play with here ...'). They all have sippy-cups full of Oros and packets of Marie Biscuits or Lemon Creams. Liesl sends the nanny in lilac to change Leon's nappy ('Don't forget to use lots of Fissan ...'). The nanny in lilac knows where the bathroom is. She has been here on these 'Daar's Werk' visits before.

Annette mixes a bottle of formula and passes it to the nanny in blue. 'Where's Polla? I'm dying for a cup of tea, Evey.'

'Not here.' Evelyn stays near the windows.

'Some of her ginger beer would be even better ...'

Evelyn turns her back on Annette's red lips and purple eye shadow.

'How is Edvard? I'm sorry we've been too busy to visit for a while. This farm really is quite a distance, isn't it?' That is Liesl speaking. 'I brought some banana bread ... Sana is very good at making banana bread, I just don't have time for baking any more. Shall I ask her to slice it up?'

'We haven't seen you and Edvard at church for a long time?' Now Mariska, playing the Dominee's wife.

'Have you heard Alta is expecting again?' Annette says. 'And her first one such a handful.'

Liesl shoots her a look, puts a finger to her lips. Annette shrugs, so what!

Evelyn parts the curtains and looks out into the glare.

'You won't believe what Petrus asked his Pa, at breakfast yesterday. It was so cute, I could've just eaten him up. He said, "Pa, how come the sheep get to play outside all day when I have to stay in the house and do what Mama tells me?"' Liesl again, with a small laugh.

Evelyn finds that if she stares out at the horizon where the sun is shimmering so bright she has to screw up her eyes, she can make the buzzing in her head loud enough to block out the voices.

But now Annette is right in front of her.

'Here Evelyn, hold Francie. You always were useless at Home Economics ... I'll make the tea. Come Sana, bring that banana bread. A nursing woman is always hungry, that's what my Ma says, and it's true hey!'

Annette thrusts her baby at Evelyn. As far as she is concerned, Evelyn heard her say the last time they visited, it's high time Evelyn got over her loss, women lose babies all the time. And this is Annette's mission again today. Holding a baby will help Evelyn. Help kick-start those maternal hormones. And if there was ever the cutest, most beautiful, sweetest, most adorable baby in the whole-wide-world, it is Francie. She will surely do the trick.

But Evelyn side-steps Annette and her Francie. 'We out of tea,' she says. 'And ginger-beer. Coffee also.'

Evelyn wonders how long it will take them to go. They are giving her peculiar looks and beginning to bicker among themselves. She is dying to pee, but doesn't want to leave the room, doesn't want to give them the opportunity of consulting one another about what they should do now.

'God, it's hot. And this wind is really getting on my nerves,' Liesl says, pulling her elasticised, strapless top away from her body, and letting it snap back. 'Oh sorry Mariska, I know ... the Lord's name. You'll have to ask Joachim to say an extra prayer for me. Evey, tell Edvard to get you some air conditioning in here. It's not that expensive any more. Ludewijk had one installed at the beginning of summer. Ag, I forgot, this side of Fraserburg isn't connected to Eskom yet. Jesus, you really are out in the bundu here hey!'

'I think that top is tasteless on a married woman' says Mariska, her own pretty floral shirt buckled over engorged breasts, and sticking between her shoulder blades, sweat stains creeping from her arm pits. 'Heavens,' she says, 'I'm dying for something to drink, but I daren't move now, this poplap is just falling asleep.'

'Shame on you, Laurie, girls don't play with cars! Give that truck back to Petrus, he had it first!' says Liesl, slapping Laurie's hands and making her cry louder. 'You might have to dress like a Dominee's wife, but I don't,' she says to Mariska above the din.

'Didn't I tell you this would be a waste of time?'' Annette hisses to them both, just loud enough for Evelyn to hear.

When they are gone, muttering never again, never, and leaving bits of Marie biscuit, a crocheted blanket, a leaking sippy-cup and a few scattered toys across the floor in their haste, Evelyn goes outside to stand in the wind. The laundry flap-flaps on the line. There is nothing pretty hanging on it. Nothing pretty or pale or soft or smelling of Elizabeth Anne Baby Shampoo. Those things are all wrapped and put away. There is nothing but socks, underpants, collared khaki shirts and shorts on her wash-line. Evelyn takes a detour past it and heads towards the kopjie. High above her, SAA's mid-day flight arcs across the sky pulling a trail of white towards Cape Town.

★

Kate takes over the driving. This was part of the country you never knew about until you found yourself in the middle of it. After a few hours of Karoo veld the rest of the world simply ceased to exist. It had been exactly the same the first time she came here to do field work at the Gansfontein Palaeo Surface, all those years ago.

Kilometre after kilometre, it always seemed as if you were making no progress. Finally Evelyn points out Fraserburg ahead of them, a shadow in the flat landscape, a spire, and then the buildings come into view.

They turn into Voortrekker Street and drive slowly up it.

★

Kate leaves Gansfontein to do some shopping and have the spare wheel repaired. While they're busy with it, she fills the Cruiser with diesel, checks the oil and water, puts air in the tyres. She is aware of people watching her. Maybe I should have changed out of my End Conscription Campaign T-shirt, she thinks.

An Isuzu bakkie drives in and stops at the other side of the pump. A burly man gets out, slams the door. Standard issue khaki shirt and shorts, rugby socks and veldskoen. His hair is cut very short. His face, neck and arms are thick and sun-burnt. He gives loud orders to the petrol jockey, then crosses the street to the bottle store.

Charming, thinks Kate. Another fine Karoo specimen.

A woman sits in the cab. Kate doesn't look twice as she walks past her on the way to the ladies room.

But the woman is standing at the basin when Kate comes out of the loo. Her face is slightly bloated, like someone with the mumps, and she still has her sunglasses on. Kate smiles politely, and indicates she wants to wash her hands.

'Excuse me.' she says.

The woman doesn't move out of the way. 'It's me, Kate. Evelyn,' she says. 'It is you, isn't it? Kate, from Fish Hoek?'

Kate nods.

'I'm Evelyn. Eve. You called me Eve. Remember?' The woman's English is clumsy. 'I ...' she begins, then stops.

A man's voice is calling her from outside. A car door slams.

She holds out a piece of paper.

Kate takes it reluctantly.

'Please ...' she says.

'Evey!' the voice is louder than the revving.

Evelyn turns before opening the door, 'Please Kate. Please come.'

In the minutes it takes for Kate to pocket the slip of paper and turn on the tap to wash her hands, thinking crazy woman, she remembers: Eve. Evelyn. The girl who bunked singing in the Republic Day rehearsals at the Good Hope Centre with her, back when they were both in high school. 1980? 1981? They had met in a public toilet that time too. Kate wrenches the door open and runs outside.

The Isuzu bakkie drives down the road, slides through the stop street, and turns left.

★

The Good Hope Centre's main hall is a vast concrete dome filled with tiered seating. The seating is filled with school children in different coloured uniforms, all practising their songs for tomorrow's Republic Day ceremony. Tomorrow, everyone has to wear white, blue or orange, depending on where their school is seated. Everyone from Kate's school has to wear orange.

In the middle of the hall is a raised platform covered with a red carpet. That is where President Botha and his wife Elize will sit with the other dignitaries, Kate supposes. She looks around, wishing she had never joined the choir, wishing she didn't have to be a stripe in the South African flag. She asks if she can go to the toilet.

'Be quick Kate, our turn is straight after Van Riebeek High is finished.' says Mr Kendrick.

Kate looks for the furthest women's toilet she can find, pushes the door open. There is a smell of vomit. A girl is sitting against the back wall, head down on her bent knees, sobbing. Kate ducks into a cubicle, hoping the crying girl will go away, but she is still there when Kate comes out.

'You okay?' Kate doesn't recognise the girl's uniform. 'Are you okay?' she asks again.

The girl mumbles something Kate doesn't quite get. Afrikaans.

'Should I call your teacher?'

At that, the girl looks up. 'No!' she says. 'I'm fine.'

'You don't look fine. Your face ... is a mess.' Kate gets some toilet paper and hands it to her. 'Here.'

The girl blows her nose. 'It's just ... my Ouma died on the weekend, but Ma wouldn't let me stay home. She said I had to come to this stupid festival, that Mr Badenhorst, the Headmaster, told her the whole school was depending on me to make them proud.' She put her head down again, 'The funeral is now, two-o'-clock.'

Kate sits down next to her. She thinks of her own granny who is such a pain in the arse that it would be nice to be rid of her and her Sunday visits, but decides it would be inappropriate to say so.

'Where you from?' she says instead.

Evelyn is from some dorpie in the Northern Cape, Kate has never heard of. Yes, she is in Matric (Kate could guess that from the braid on the edge of her blazer). Yes, she is a prefect – head girl in fact. Her dad had been a farmer, but he died when she was twelve, and they had to move into town. Her Ma works in the post office. Ouma Elsa always lived with them.

Kate tells Evelyn her parents are academics. That they work at UCT. That she is expected to be an A-student, but would rather surf, or play hockey, than study. She has no chance of being head girl when she gets to Matric, let alone a prefect.

'Let's bunk the rest of this stupid rehearsal,' she says

Kate nicks the Out of Order / Buite Werking sign from the men's toilet and props it up against the women's toilet door. 'No-one will come in here now.'

They take turns dragging on a Benson & Hedges.

Evelyn gets light-headed. She is not used to cigarettes. She sings a few lines of 'Sarie Marais'. It is, was, her Ouma's favourite song.

'Do you have a boy-friend.'

'Me? No.'

'I do.' Evelyn says. 'But he's in the army.'

When they have finished their second cigarette, they creep out of the toilets and hide under the grandstands. They can hear the singing. The rehearsal is in full swing. There is a rumble overhead, everyone is standing. They sing 'Uit die blou van onse hemel', all the schools together.

Kate and Evelyn know they will be in trouble for bunking, especially Evelyn. She is the lead soprano in her choir and has been selected to sing with Mimi Coertse, tomorrow night. It was a great honour, everyone said so.

'I don't care.' Evelyn says. 'They can make me come here, but they can't make me sing. And anyway, it doesn't matter any more. I am in big trouble already.' She cries a little more, 'for my Ouma' she says, and tells Kate to light another cigarette.

Kate hears afterwards that Evelyn has been expelled. She overhears Mr Kendrick, the choir teacher, tell Miss Martins, the music teacher, while they wait outside the principal's office for her own reckoning.

'There was a huge stink. The headmaster said he felt publicly humiliated because the girl went AWOL when she was supposed to sing for P.W., never mind it was only a rehearsal!'

'It's a bit extreme,' says Miss Martins, 'to expel a pupil in her Matric year because she bunked a rehearsal? That's the problem with Afrikaners – they are so extreme.'

Kate's own punishment is a written warning and a ban on playing first team hockey for the rest of term.

At home, her parents look at her worriedly across the dining room table. Her mother comes into her room after supper while her Dad is washing up, props herself up on the window sill and asks as carefully as she can, what possessed her to sneak off with a girl she didn't know, in the middle of a Republic Day rehearsal – and smoke cigarettes?

'An Afrikaans girl from Fraserburg?'

'Such an unlikely friend?'

'I didn't know you smoked, Kate!'

*

It is only when she is back at Gansfontein, that Kate thinks to look at the slip of paper she had put in her pocket.

Verlatenkloof off the Jakkalsfontein Road

Nothing else. No name. No telephone number. No directions to help her find the place.

*

Kate watches carefully for the turn-off, a farm track leaving the gravel road at a diagonal. She must be close now, judging by the distance she has already covered and the low rise of hills in the distance, a rumple in this otherwise well ironed piece of earth.

She stops the Cruiser for a minute, to rest. All around her the land lies bleached. Everything is still. Not even a black-headed sheep picking at the soutbossies for company. She gets out and walks towards a small mound. In amongst the scrub, the curve of an old bakoond, and remnants of a stone wall, mud plaster still visible in places. She picks up a rusted bit of iron, a buckle of some kind, from a harness perhaps, and a teaspoon, nickel-plated silver tarnished beyond redemption. She pockets her treasure and heads back to the Cruiser. There can't be much further to go. It is almost mid-day and shadowless. The rumple is closer now, like a blanket tossed carelessly to one side, an unmade bed. Twin kopjies.

She shifts into a lower gear, feeling the incline's demand, pulling steeply up and up, then into a tight corner that forces her to slow down, and suddenly she is there. Suddenly the fences, and a cattle grate, a sullen wind-pump with a cement dam, a clump of blue gums on the far side, fruit trees of some sort, and the farm house squatting in a yard of gravel, next to an odd assortment of sheds. She has found Verlatenkloof.

*

Edvard crawls out from under the bakkie when he hears the car. Wipes his hands against the legs of his blue overalls. He knows trouble is coming. The south wind brings nothing but trouble, and it has been blowing these last few days like nobody's business. Edvard is not expecting anybody. Could be some old friend of Evelyn's turning up out of the woodwork, he thinks. They used to be here a lot. Yes, it's just some woman. Bugger if he's going to stop what he's doing for a woman.

Edvard climbs back under the bakkie. Shit, man. Could've had Jaapie check this engine out on Thursday, but no, the fucking bakkie has to wait till they're back on the farm to break down.

Evelyn is refolding the pretty baby things into their tissue paper when she hears the car come into the yard.

It *was* Kate at the Caltex Garage. She had come.

Evelyn pries the gold band from her finger and lays it on top of the little pile. She places them in the top drawer next to a piece of glass from the bedroom window Edvard smashed last week, and slides the drawer closed.

She picks up her handbag. In it is her identity book, a photo of herself as a little girl with Ma, Pa and Ouma Elsa, a few sewejaartjies from the west kopjie, and her wallet. She is outside, ready to go, before Kate even climbs out of the Cruiser.

Polla waves goodbye.

Incognito

Her name is Elizabeth, and if you are tempted to call her Liz, or worse still Beth or Betsy, don't. Her style may be bohemian and her morals careless, but it doesn't mean you can mess with her name.

This is the day Elizabeth has been wanting ever since adolescence, and finally it is here. Finally there are only a few more steps down the strip of faded carpet, a few words to repeat, a kiss to exchange.

The sun is summer bright. Early risers leave the beach, vacating their parking spots for those foolish enough to lie in. Most of the congregation sprawl outside in the chapel's wall-hugging shade, unable to fit into the little, thatched rondavel, musty from want of use.

The bride pauses at the door, a sudden posy picked from the neighbour's garden in her hands. Her dress, a white cotton shift. Her feet bare, with sand between unpolished toes. At the other end of the worn carpet stands Teddy, tall and skinny. Bones poking out in sharp exclamations where shoulders, elbows and knees should be. Big hair spills across his boyish face. He smiles down from an open necked shirt and a gaily coloured waistcoat Elizabeth hasn't seen before.

Teddy has a delightful surname, as if to compensate for the embarrassment of his first. Feast. In her mind she sees banquets, parties and endless celebration. Images of goblets, platters laden with food, music, minstrels and medieval castles. Feast, an abundant, generous name. One she could live with.

Elizabeth's own surname is a trail of austerity and oppression she has dragged behind her for twenty five years. Almost as restrictive to her as it has been to millions of others, she avoids it as often as she can, never introduces herself as anything other than 'Elizabeth'. She says it with a firmness that brooks no further questions, and answers to nothing more. And though you may think she should be used to it by now, adult that she is, she is not. Some women can't abide disclosing their age. Elizabeth can't abide disclosing her name.

Elizabeth sees Daneel as she walks the few steps down the aisle with gentle old Prof Wilkes, substituting for the father she is no longer talking to. She wonders at Daneel's presence. This brother of hers who disowned her so many times. Perhaps Ma persuaded him? Or perhaps he's practising the forgiveness he preaches as a Dominee? He looks ridiculous, she thinks, in that black suit and tie, so out of place among the T-shirts and beach dresses.

'If there is anyone here, who knows of any reason why these two should not be joined in Holy Matrimony, let them speak now or forever hold their peace,' says Father Michael, hardly glancing up. Then turning to Teddy he says, 'Now then ...'

'Excuse me, Dominee,' cuts in Daneel. 'Excuse me,' he says again, 'Father,' and clears his throat. 'But I must tell you, you must know, wat ek wou sê is ... it's that you, that she, is not of our blood. She is adopted. Aangeneem. Ja. I have papers now to show it. Ek is jammer. But he,' pointing now at Teddy, 'he must know it, has the right to know who he is marrying. You must know it too, Elizabeth. Pa and Ma should have told you themselves, a long time ago already.'

Teddy puts his arm around Elizabeth, but she shakes it off, staring at her mother.

'Yes. You were born to a Helen Smith, of 44 Vista St, East London, it says so here, and adopted into our family at two weeks of age. I have the papers to prove it.' He waves a wad in the air.

'Smith?' Elizabeth sounds out the anonymity of the name; tastes the blandness in her mouth. Hundreds and thousands of people called Smith ... must be the commonest surname in the English world, she thinks. Elizabeth Smith. It's about as incognito as you can get.

'Is it true, Ma?' Elizabeth turns to the only woman wearing a hat, seated a little off to the side, not knowing anyone but Daneel, and with no-one to reserve a front row seat for her as they should.

Her mother stands up, sways a little on her black high heels and abruptly sits down again. Her perfectly made up face pales. Her mouth opens, but no words come out. Her large bosom, embossed in a shrimp coloured silk blouse, heaves.

'Is dit waar, Ma?' Elizabeth asks a little louder, shrugging Teddy's hand off her shoulder more impatiently this time.

Her mother nods a slow, almost imperceptible, yes. And still not meeting her daughter's gaze says, 'Maar Betsy, jy is nog altyd my kind.'

Elizabeth stiffens.

Teddy reaches for her again. 'Babe ...'

But Elizabeth has no further need of his attention. She steps out of his reach. 'My name isn't Betsy,' she whispers. 'And as it turns out,' she looks over at Daneel, 'it isn't Verwoerd either.'

Unsettled

un·set·tled
adj.
Lacking order or stability
Worried and uneasy
Liable to change; unpredictable
Not yet resolved
Having no settlers or inhabitants

– oxforddictionaries.com

When Sue wakes up, she's not sure if it's night or morning. Nor is she entirely sure where she is. The smell is familiar, the feel of the sheets, the heft of the duvet. Even the dark (no street lights) and the lack of noise suggest she is waking in the same place she went to bed. These things are familiar, yet she gropes about for clues to anchor herself. She feels beneath her body the rim of the depression she has worn in the mattress. She feels the heat from Dominic's body curled away from her. Her own bed. Her own home. But she knows too, that she has been away. Far away.

For a moment or two she lingers in that other place where there are always cars; always lights; people on the street. She sees them bundled up in coats, scarves and hats, heads bent against the wind. She sees herself, one of them, waiting to cross the street. She is wearing a cream wool coat, very stylish. It covers the top of her long boots. She recognises the boots. The light changes and she moves, walking between a man with a small dog snarled up in its leash, two young women, a group of teenagers with wires coming out of their ears, and another man who towers over the others. It is this man she notices most. She wants to be with him. There is something compelling, something that presses at her to follow him. She wants to see where he is going. She thinks maybe she is supposed to go there too. Perhaps they have a mutual friend, a mutual engagement? There is a look about him.

The man is carrying a huge bunch of vark lilies, their thick juicy stems leave silvery tracks on the black of his coat. The white of the flowers is the white of snow under a bright sun. It hurts her eyes. Hang on. There is something wrong in this scene. You don't buy vark lilies at a city florist. No. You pick them yourself in swampy areas or buy them from bergies at street corners. But only for funerals. They are unlucky otherwise. Like opals. Sue wants to ask him whose funeral he is going to, and where-ever did he find those flowers? She calls to him. Her voice comes out a mangled, dry mouthed gargle;

'Aarrck.'

He is walking fast now, he is getting away. She remembers a name, his name perhaps, and she calls again, frantic she will lose sight of him.

'AARRRCK.'

'Hey,' mumbles Dominic, 'hey now. Sssh. You're dreaming again.'

He puts an arm over her and curls around her body. It's how they liked to sleep, once upon a time, pressed up against one another like two spoons. They don't sleep much like that any more.

Sue eases out from under his arm, gets up and soft foots across the floor in her sheepskin slippers, through the tiny lounge, the kitchen and into the bathroom. She really ought to drink less tea. The kitchen clock says six thirty. She might as well set off now. She knows the way. She'll take the dog. It will be light in half an hour and she can be home before the kids are awake. They like her to be home when they wake. And when they go to sleep.

There are birds calling now, a cape robin, a batis, still tentative, but awake. The pale gravel crunches beneath her running shoes. Maybe she'll see an owl? Sue shakes out her arms and rolls her shoulders. She feels displaced, oddly bodiless. In the dark, she knows the mountains are waiting. She knows their exact position, their orientation, their expression. She knows which peak will be touched first, and how the mantle of sun will trail down the slopes lighting up the dark green of row upon row of pine. But all of this is hidden now.

She turns off the forestry road and onto a seldom used Jeep track. The long grass between the wheel tracks is thick with dew. It *thwaks* against her bare legs and soaks her shoes. The dog sets the pace and chooses the route. Or that's how it seems to Sue. She sees nothing, feels nothing, only vaguely conscious of the heaviness dissolving in her thighs and the ease of her breathing as she reaches a long contour. She is not aware of the change from plantation into fynbos. Nor of the light which is trickling into the valley. She is somewhere else. Her body runs on past the rooiels grove. She picks her way across a stream, and the dog stops to drink. Her body feels the jar of a sharp descent. Sue is too busy trying to name a location, the place far away she has just come back from, and a person; who was it she'd gone to see? And who was the man she tried to call?

The sun has not yet reached her garden by the time she gets back to her own front gate. She must remember to feed Rosie's rabbit or it will surely die. Die. Somebody has died. Sue pulls the dark shadow of her dream behind her and into the house. Dominic is up. In the kitchen. Making tea. She stands on one leg, stretching. Watches him.

'Nice run?' he asks.

'Not much of a welcome home,' Sue says.

'You've only been gone an hour or two. What do you want, flowers? A kiss?' He plants one on the top of her bent head. Dominic generally wakes up cheerful.

'Is that all? Haven't I been away for weeks and just come back? It feels like I've been away. Far away.'

'You should eat before you go, a banana at least. You're probably a bit hypoglycaemic.' Dominic pushes a mug of tea across the table in her direction. 'Or maybe it's your dream. You were shouting in your sleep again.' But no, he couldn't decipher the words. Didn't catch a name.

'I was somewhere cold. Somewhere I didn't go out much. A big city, much bigger than Cape Town, and colder. Somewhere like London, or Paris, or Amsterdam maybe.' Sue used to travel to London, Paris and Amsterdam for work before she gave up all that to take her writing more seriously. 'And someone was dying. I can't figure out who. There was a man. A really tall, black man. He was carrying a bunch of vark lilies. Of all things.'

Dominic smiles fondly at her and picks up the *Weekend Argus*. 'Write a story about it. You were complaining you didn't have any inspiration for your next piece.'

But Sue isn't listening. She has taken her tea and a roll of toilet paper with her into the garden. She blows her nose savagely. The lawn needs mowing and the lavender needs cutting back. She wanders over to the stone bird bath and looks among the bushes for the first sign of spring. Not a bulb showing. Nothing. Of course not, it's not yet mid winter.

Sue makes for the back of the garden to a pre-cast cement bench beneath a pompom tree. There are three metal hearts hanging on thin beaded strings in the tree. She's hung them there each year without saying anything to Dominic. It's her own small memorial for baby. She and Dominic had fought terribly while trying to plant that tree. Sue taps the hearts gently with her forefinger and watches the glass beads glint as they spin.

The children find her there, sloughing sleep from their small shoulders as they wander over the wet lawn in their pyjamas. They have always, thank God, been good sleepers. Benjamin holds his sister by one hand, a book in the other.

'Mama,' he calls, 'read us a story.'

The children snuggle up onto her lap and lean into her body.

'You've been crying,' says Rosie. She doesn't ask why. That's how it is with Rosie, even at five. She sees things.

Sue contemplates asking her daughter if she knows anyone who died in the night. But she knows it would be ridiculous, wouldn't it? She ruffles Rosie's hair.

'I had a bad dream,' she says, 'that's all.'

'Me too,' Rosie says.

'Poor baby. What about?'

'I dreamt you went away and didn't come back.'

Sue squeezes Rosie tight. 'I went for a run early, but I'm here now.'

'Saskia's mother went away and didn't come back. That's why she has to go to after-care every day. Teacher Lorraine told us,' says Rosie.

'Read,' says Benjy.

The book Benjamin has is one she's read a hundred times, *Warthog and Leopard*. While she reads the story of the tightrope - walking warthog, her mind drifts back to her dream. There had been someone else there. Someone who knew the place well. Someone who could give directions when unpacking the dishwasher. Someone who knew where to find the coffee plunger, the spaghetti spoon. Someone young, who looked just like ...

'Mom, you're not reading p-r-o-p-e-r-l-y.'

'Warthog and Leopard are never separated again. They become famous performers and star in circuses all over the world. They live as best friends for ever and ever after.'

'The end,' says Benjamin.

'Yes Benjy, the end.' Best not to leave anything out.

Rosie sits on the little wooden stool and watches Sue while she showers. Sue wishes she would go away. She makes the water as hot as she can bear, trying to scald the shadow that has attached itself to her heels, to burn it off. She will not carry it around on such a beautiful day.

'Now your bum is red too,' Rosie says, as Sue towels dry.

They eat a breakfast of raw oats, almonds and grated apples. The kids eat Oatees, the standard Saturday concession to an otherwise healthy diet.

'I'll be back by three, three-thirty,' Sue says. 'I'll pick up some milk and bread on my way home. Maybe a DVD?'

But Dominic says he has a proposal to finish for Monday and will need to work through the night, seeing as he's looking after the kids all day. He says it sweetly, but Sue feels the accusation.

'Remember to come back, Mommy,' says Rosie waving, as Sue reverses down the drive way.

There are only twelve people in the room, mostly white, middle-aged women like herself. Two so-called Coloured women and two Muslim men. And Andile. Andile catches her eye and winks. They've worked together in many platforms over the years – and called it many things. Diversity Dialogues is the current favoured phrase. People generally find it a lot less threatening than Racism. Or Sexism. But, it seems, not a whole lot more interesting. Today Sue is not a facilitator, she is just one of the twelve, a parent at Oakdale Primary.

'It's June sixteenth,' Andile says.

Some people nod knowingly. Others look around the room as if seeking a clue to the significance of the date.

'Youth Day. Thirty seventh anniversary of the student uprising in Soweto. It seems an auspicious date for the parent body to begin working on issues of diversity. Let's begin with introductions. I am Andile Sithole, from the Institute of Peace and Reconciliation.'

Does he ever question the value of all this? Whether it really makes any difference, Sue wonders.

'Please choose an object from the tray in the middle of the circle,' Andile says, 'any object that appeals to you in some way, and use it to introduce yourself, say why you are here, perhaps a little about what you were doing this day in 1976.'

Sue shakes herself. Recalls her attention from that cold, far away place back into the room. She tries to concentrate on what the woman on the other side of the circle is saying about growing up blissfully unaware of anything untoward going on in the country. The woman has chosen a box of matches from the pile of objects and is waving it about like a kid with a rattle.

'And I don't even know any Blacks or Coloureds,' she concludes.

The next person in the circle has an old photo album on her lap. It is not from the pile on the floor, but something she has brought with her. She opens it and turns the pages, not looking up. It bulges with newspaper clippings.

'My sisters and I started compiling this album in 1976. I was seventeen at the time, in standard nine, that's grade eleven, right? We kept every article or picture we could find on Sharpeville, and when it spread down here, about the local school boycotts too.' She looks up and hands the album to the man next to her.

'Yes,' he says, turning a page as if it were a holy book. 'Yes.'

'Every year, my sisters, brothers and me, we get together, on June sixteenth, to look at the album. And to remember. We've tried explaining it to our kids. We try to explain what it was like being at school in the seventies. What it was like being a Coloured person then. But it's so foreign to them. We could just as well be talking about the ancient Greeks and Romans. But it still lives in us. It ... haunts us.' The woman with the album has tears sliding down her face. The man sitting next to her puts a hand on her shoulder.

'Sorry,' she says, 'I'm feeling a bit emotional. Oh and my name is Merel. Merel Brown. Once, by the way, I sent out a group email at work and by mistake, added a 'y' at the end of my name. That's how I feel in this country sometimes you know, Merely Brown.'

Only Merely Brown laughs. Some of the others have odd looks on their faces, like dogs caught at something. They are all quiet for a while. Then the next person goes. And the next.

'I must have just started primary school in '76,' says Sue. It is her turn to speak, though she doesn't yet know what to say. 'I knew nothing about Sharpeville.'

She holds a miniature Paddington Bear in her hands. Paddington Bear holds a suitcase in his. 'I chose this bear because he reminds me of a university friend, a very close friend, though I lost touch with her after we graduated. I heard many years later that she had emigrated.' Sue has not thought of Adi for ages. Why now? 'In the white community, everybody knows somebody who has emigrated, so the news just kind of washed over me at the time. But after a while it really got to me, *really* got to me. She was passionate about this country, she sacrificed so much. Why would she go? Just when Mandela was finally about to become president?'

Why, she thinks, did Adi have to leave? And what the hell am I still doing here? She swallows hard.

'She was like a sister to me for the short time we knew each other, like a twin. We were born on the same day of the same year. We started school in the same year, reached high school in the same year. In 1985 I wrote my Matric exams under military protection – there had been bomb threats, school kids were rioting in other parts of town. Adi was part of those riots. While I wrote my final papers in my nice, whites only, government high school, she was arrested and detained. They kept her inside, detention without trial, for six months. We only lived thirteen kilometres apart, but really, we lived in different worlds.'

Merely Brown nods, so does the man next to her. The woman with sinus problems passes a tissue along the circle to Sue. Andile clears his throat, spreads his hands. Somebody gets up and puts the kettle on. Time for a break.

Sue gets home to an empty house. There is a note from Dominic. He has taken the children to visit his dad. They'll be home at six. She has two and a half unexpected hours to herself. Sue goes into the study and lifts down an old photo album. The cover has a picture of wild horses galloping along an orange beach. A few photos slide out of the pages where the glue no longer has any stick. They are not the ones she is looking for. At the back of the album are her graduation photographs. There is the one of her in her white dress and black graduation gown with its purple hood, standing with her parents. Her father, in suit and tie, is grinning madly and holding her certificate in a victory salute, as if it were his own. And there is the one of her with Mary and Adi. She and Adi are arm in arm, laughing. Mary is slightly to one side, holding her graduation gown open to show what's underneath: a yellow, black and green striped tunic and a sign pinned to the inside of her gown which reads, Free Nelson Mandela. Mary stood on stage, just after being capped, and opened her gown to the audience. The polite clapping had gone wild, at least in the front of Jameson Hall, where the graduates sat.

Sue peels the photo from its place and carries it to her desk. She switches on her laptop and waits for it to warm up, watches all the little icons flicker ever so slightly as if waking. She logs on to Facebook and types in Adi's full name under search-for-friend. She scrolls through the options Facebook offers, but can't find anyone like her Adi. Maybe she's changed names? She adds the University of Cape Town, but has no other way of limiting the field. After Russell's death, Adeela went underground. Sue knows nothing more recent about her, nothing that will help trace her in cyberspace.

She tries again, this time typing in Mary Taylor. She adds UCT and Women's Legal Centre, the last place Mary worked before leaving for Canada. It has been more than ten years since they'd last had contact. Sue scrolls through the Mary Taylors with Facebook accounts. There is one living in Toronto that catches her eye. The photograph is of a child building a snowman, her daughter perhaps? Sue had heard that Mary had had a daughter. Who would've told her? She clicks on that Mary Taylor. Yes it's her, it must be.

There are only a few photos, mostly of snow scenes, and one of her, half facing the camera, at a distance. It's hard to make a positive identification, but the page has links to the Institute for a Democratic Alternative in South Africa and The Women's Legal Centre. It gives her occupation as professor at the University of Toronto, Faculty of Law.

Sue sends a friend request. Then she tries Google. She finds nothing for Adi, but a slew of links for Mary, mostly academic journals, and one with her University contact details.

From:	*Sue Key*
To:	*Mary Taylor*
Subject:	*making contact*
Date:	*June 16th 2013*
Time:	*16h35*

Dear Mary
Today is Youth Day. June 16. I have been thinking of you and Adi all day, wondering where you both are, how you are and what you are doing. How is it that we are so out of touch? I saw a photo on Facebook of a woman who looks like you, with a little girl? Is that you, is she yours? If I have the right Mary, I would love to hear from you.
Sue

From: *Mary Taylor*
To: *Sue Key*
Subject: *RE: making contact*
Date: *June 16th 2013*
Time: *17h03*

Darling Sukey hello.
Is it really you? I could hardly believe it when I saw your
name pop into my in-box. I have been thinking of you a lot
recently, not least because Adi's daughter contacted me out of
the blue just last week, asking after you.

I am living in Toronto and yes, I have a nine year
old daughter, Wanda. Do you remember Roberto? From
Mozambique? Well he's Wanda's dad and we still have
an on/off thing going, which is pretty much all you can
have when living on two separate continents. Roberto hates
Canada. And I just can't live in Africa any more.

Adi lives in New York. I met up with her again at a
conference on, wait for it, Women's Rights and HIV/Aids a
few years back, and we've stayed in contact since then. She
was one of the keynote speakers, and so was I. So neither of
us has totally abandoned the cause, you see. Totally weird to
see each other again. We spent a wonderful evening together,
and I got to meet her daughter, a really amazing kid. She
has her mother's eyes. As you ask, how is it possible we have
grown so far apart?

I see from your email address that you are still in South
Africa. You always said you would stay. And so you have.
Despite everything. Are you still with Dominic? How about
kids, do you have any? Do write back and tell me everything.
What a wonderful way this has been to start my day.
Love
Mary xx
PS: I am emailing your details to Adi's daughter right now.

From: *Lilly Khan*
To: *Sue Key*
Subject: *RE:RE: making contact*
Date: *June 16th 2013*
Time: *17h50*

Dear Sue
This is Lilly, Adeela's daughter. I got your email address from
Mary Taylor. My mom has been talking a lot about you and
Mary in the last few months. I know you three were really
close friends in the years before she left South Africa. I know
that was a long time ago and that she hasn't had any contact
with you since then, though she is in touch occasionally with
Mary. She's says you are probably angry with her for leaving
the way she did and not ever contacting you. She says you
were like sisters back then, and that she misses you more than
anything. My mom is dying of cancer – she probably doesn't
have all that long left. I don't know how to put it except
straight like that. I'm sorry if it's a shock. My mom really
wants to see you and Mary again. She wants to have you
both in the same room, at the same time. And she wants me
to meet you. I know it is just a fantasy she has, and that it's
a lot to ask, but I'd like to make it real. So I am writing to
ask if you would consider making the trip to New York, say
in September, if that suits you? We are able to pay your fare
and would have you stay here with us in our apartment. We
live in Brooklyn. I hope you are not too shocked or offended
by this request. I know you will have to think about it before
replying, but please Sukey, please think about it, even if you
are still hurt or mad with my Mom.
Got to go now
Lilly
PS: Mom doesn't know I am emailing you. I don't want to
disappoint her if things don't work out.

It's dark outside. The dog will want feeding. And the rabbit – she mustn't forget the rabbit again. There is still laundry hanging on the line. Sue knows she should light a fire before it gets any colder. She should start on the supper – the kids will be hungry when they get back.

When Dominic arrives home, the house is all dark. The dog leaps up at him, runs circles around his legs. He opens the door and goes into the house, the kids asleep in the car. There are no lights on, no fire. No smell of cooking. He finds her at her desk, in a blue pool of light. She turns to look at him as he comes into the room.

'What's going on?' he says. 'You okay?'

'It's Adeela,' she says, 'She's dying. That's what my dream is about.'

By Any Other Name

I. Adeela

It was the girls' idea, getting them together, Lilly's and Vanezu's. They set it all up, booked a table for four, organised their respective parents.

'Can't you wear a dress rather?' Lilly fussed at her. 'It's Eataly we're going to, Mom, near Union Square. Think fancy.'

Adeela stands in her underwear, hair still wet, a favourite pair of jeans in her hand. It's hard to please a teenager, and though she generally tries to be accommodating, draws the line at dresses.

'Nope. I don't do dresses, not even for you,' she says, 'not even for a blind date.'

'Okay then, how about this?' Lilly takes down a heavily embroidered silk shirt Adeela hardly ever wears. 'This will zhoosh your jeans up a little, and with my big silver earrings and your long boots, you'll look all right. It's not a date exactly. We just think it's a good idea you two finally meet.'

Victor and Adeela like each other immediately. Though they avoid any talk of nationality, there is an ease between them, a familiarity, a feeling of belonging. The girls buzz around, filling the slightest pause with chit-chat. They speak about their favourite New York haunts. The wonders of living in a first-world city. Lilly loves the Museum of Modern Art best,

Vanezu, Soho. Adeela the bookshops, and Victor the people.

'If you'd asked me twenty, ten, even five years ago, I would have told you I hated Americans and all things American. But somehow, in their own country, they aren't so bad,' he says.

Now here is Victor, she knows it's him without turning around. He crosses the small space between the front door and her chair in only nine paces, bends down to kiss her.

'I'm happy to see you looking so well this morning,' he says. It's a lie, but he feels compelled to say it. He pulls up a footstool and sits at her feet. Still Adeela has to tilt her head up a little to see his face.

He takes off his steel-rimmed glasses and carefully polishes the lenses, puts them on, and with a little nudge, edges them into place. He watches her come back into focus, but finds she looks the same as when he first came into the room. The joints in her fingers are swollen, the skin along the top of her hands taut over the bones. Her arms limp on the side-rests of the old corduroy-covered rocking chair are as spindly as the topmost branches of the tree at her window. She is wearing an old grey cardigan of fine wool, and on it she, or more likely Lilly, has pinned a white, heart-shaped brooch made from springbok hide. He gave it to her, last Valentine's or the one before. The space where her breasts were is concave beneath a cotton T-shirt. Like sinkholes, he thinks, where the earth has suddenly collapsed, swallowing whatever was there – houses, people, animals, trees – whole lives disappearing in an instant.

'Your tree is especially beautiful this time of year.' Victor nods towards the elm, takes a sip of the tea Lilly fixed them before going out. He wishes Adeela would dress like a dying woman, cover her deformity with a robe or a blanket for Christ's sake. Wear a scarf or a hat of some kind over the fine hair that pushes so pathetically from her scalp. To Victor's complete surprise, he begins to cry. First the rise of heat up his cheeks, then the tell-tale burning at the back of his eyes. The blurring of his vision. God, this woman could always reduce him to an almost unbearably sweet state of rawness. He feels naked, always naked when he is with her.

They will be refugees again, Vanezu and him, when she is gone.

'I think I made a friend today. Her name's Lilly.' Victor can picture Vanezu the day she'd told him that. She sounded so formal. So hopeful. So homesick.

'Sounds positive,' he'd said. 'Sounds positive' was how he'd greeted all good news since arriving in the States. They'd only been there two months or so, and something about the place, the sheer size of it maybe, made him feel, well, cautious.

Since Adeela's diagnosis he'd given up using the word positive altogether. He and Vanezu had stopped joking about how the Americans can turn their own words inside out and upside down. It didn't seem funny any more.

Victor is usually able to stem his tears before they show; a nail pushed into the palm of a clenched fist or into the soft tip of his thumb; the removal of his spectacles, the methodical polishing of their lenses on a corner of his shirt. Then he is ready to look up, to resume the distant stance of a respected academic, the authoritative look of a father. Or in this case, the detached fondness of an ex lover. But this time, his tricks do not work. This time, almost before he knows it, Victor puts his head on Adeela's lap and sobs.

She strokes his head with a hand she doesn't fully recognise. She feels the familiar prickle of his recently shorn head under her fingers. She watches a finch flit from branch to branch before it drops two storeys down to Mr Cohen's bird feeder. It is quiet inside, just the rasp of Victor's sobbing and the slight rumble of the refrigerator as its motor kicks in across the room. The street noises seem far away.

'I used to think,' Adeela says when Victor stops crying, 'I

used to think I'd like my ashes to be buried here under the elm. It's an alien, you know, like you and me.' They sit quietly for a moment looking out at the English elm that doesn't really belong. 'Somebody probably brought this tree over from England. Somebody unwrapped the roots from the damp sacks bound around them, soil still clinging to them in great clumps, crumbling and trickling away as it dried. Someone dug a hole and planted it, a little, withered, homesick sapling, right here. Planted it, watered it, tended it. That somebody had conviction, didn't they, Victor?'

Victor doubts the tree sailed across the Atlantic with some early settler. Hell, that would make it hundreds of years old. More likely, it was grown in a nursery somewhere closer at hand. Central Park was full of elms, wasn't it?

'Do you want Vanezu to put her roots down here, Victor? Lilly has. She's never lived anywhere else. And I thought I had roots here too. I thought I was as well transplanted as that tree. But now, I'm not so sure,' Adeela chuckles. 'Anyway, old Mr Cohen won't let anybody into his yard and I don't want to make things harder for Lilly, so now I'm thinking of asking Sukey to take my ashes home with her. There's a place I used to go every Christmas when I was a kid. Maiden's Cove. Sukey knows it; she grew up near there. She can just tip them into the Atlantic. What do you think?'

Victor says nothing. He puts his head back onto her lap. It feels to Adeela as heavy as a rock. The grey spikes glint like quartzite against his black dome. And she feels it crushing her legs. Feels her legs disintegrating, turning to sand beneath the weight. She is short of breath again. Feels the weight move up to her chest. She focuses on the tree. On her breathing. The finch is back. It hops along a twig away from her, then flies off.

'I'm sorry,' Victor says, lifting his head.

Adeela looks down to find her lap as it was, not crushed, not crumbling away. Just two thin legs cased in faded blue denim. She motions for her tea which is just out of reach. He passes it to her, waits until she has a firm grip on the handle. It steadies her a little, this ancient ritual of drinking tea. Not American-style tea, but proper English tea, with milk and one sugar.

'We used to go there, to Maiden's Cove, every year on Boxing Day, until we moved away from the city.' She's speaking to Victor, but her eyes are on the tree. 'Half the neighbourhood would go. Ma would pack all our stuff: blankets, towels, shorts, warm jerseys for the trip home, into a big string bag. The rotis and sandwiches, bottles of Fanta or Coca-Cola went into plastic OK Bazaar packets. We'd walk down Constitution Street, right into Buitenkant and then along Darling, into Adderley Street, where we'd catch the bus to just past Clifton, but before you got to Camps Bay proper. Those were whites-only beaches back then.'

'Hmm,' Victor says.

'There wasn't exactly a beach at Maiden's Cove – but there was sand here and there between the rocks, and a huge tidal pool. My cousin Ryder was the only one of us who could swim. He would run along the white-painted walls and dive into the pool just before the huge waves knocked him off. It was a game the big boys played, a bit like chicken.' Adeela pauses, takes another sip of tea. Victor's mug is already empty.

'We used to explore all the nooks and crannies between those rocks, Amina, Huda and me. They were just granite boulders, but to us, they were castles, the walls studded with diamonds. We would go back one day and get those diamonds out, we promised ourselves. We would chip them out and be rich as princesses. I can't remember what Amina wanted to buy, or Huda, but I wanted roller skates, like the white girls I'd seen when the bus drove past the Sea Point Boulevard. I didn't know what they were called, nobody I knew had them, but Ryder told me.'

Adeela puts her mug down, too heavy to hold any longer. 'I have a picture of Ryder in that box. Do you want to see it?'

Victor does not want to talk about Ryder. He does not want to talk about scattering ashes. He wants to pretend this isn't happening. He wants to hurl his mug across the room, listen to it smash against the framed Matisse print, watch the tannins stain the white wall brown. He wants to fling the French windows wide open. He wants to fly with her through the gap between the apartment buildings and show her what's left of the autumn leaves, show her the skyline, the bridge, the river, the new independent book-store that's opened not three blocks away on Court Street. He wants to stop in at The Chocolate Room and have the waitress bring their favourite coffee. He wants to keep her here. He doesn't want her to go anywhere.

'Sure,' he says, feigning what, exactly? Enthusiasm for the reminiscence of a dying friend? Victor is aware of trying to rise out of his own need to be comforted. His need to talk about them as they were. He wants Adeela to say how she regrets ending their affair, regrets relegating him to a close friend. He imagines the moment she finally concedes. He imagines he can rescue her. Even from this.

'Sure,' he says again, aiming for encouraging.

The box is down on the floor, between her chair and the wall. It is a medium-size cardboard box that has been hand decorated and then varnished. On the lid, there's an amateurish portrait. It takes Victor a moment, as he stoops to pick it up, to realise that it is Adeela's face on the lid.

Adeela laughs at him. 'Good thing I usually leave painting to Lilly, hey?'

Her name is printed under the self-portrait, and a date. Her birth date. She lifts the lid and rummages about, then pulls out a newspaper cutting, slightly crisped by age, and hands it to him. *Cape Times*, 30 June 1976. There are a lot of people in the picture, mostly young, students, school-kids even, a few older people. 'Police disperse thousands of protesters,' reads the caption.

He gives the newspaper cutting back to Adeela, 'Which one is your cousin?'

Adeela is hugging her chest as if cold. Victor feels a flash of guilt for wanting to yank the door open.

'Do you need a blanket? Want to lie down?'

Adeela shakes her head. 'This one,' she says, pointing. 'And that's me just behind him.'

Victor looks again, but can only see what looks like the corner of a skirt behind the wavy-haired boy she's pointing at.

'That was the last time I saw him. He was supposed to be looking after me because the schools were closed. But Ryder said he had to go on this march, did I want to go along? There had been marches in our neighbourhood before, but Ma had always kept me home.'

Adeela stares at the grainy black-and-white picture. 'You can see,' she says, 'the clouds are down low over Table Mountain. It was really cold that day and rainy, but we still went. Ryder helped me do a double bow on my takkies before we set off up the street. They had been Elza's takkies and were still a bit too big. I loved those takkies – they were plain white canvas with a green and yellow stripe down the side of the foot to the rubber toe. They had thick rubber soles. Good for running and jumping. Ryder said we might have to do some running, so I put them on. There was a crowd gathering; we could hear the singing while we were still walking down Buitenkant Street. There was a helicopter flying low over town, and police vans. We used to call them Black Marias ... I don't know why. That made me kind of nervous. We walked with some of the other boys from Ryder's school who lived near us, bigger boys who were joking with Ryder about being the next Hector Pietersen. I had no clue who that was. I thought maybe he was a movie star. Ryder loved going to movies at the Avalon bioscope. I remember feeling quite proud that these big boys thought Ryder was going to be a star. I only found out later, much later, who Hector Pietersen was.'

Adeela stops talking. Victor takes a yellowing hand into his. The heavy silver ring swings loosely on her middle finger. He turns it the right way up so the big blue stone, the colour of Adeela's eyes, is on top. It's a ring, he knows, that belonged to her grandmother. The only thing she has ever told him about her family before now. He covers the small hand in both of his big, indecently fleshy ones, careful not to crush her.

'I had to wear shoes too small for my feet the rest of that winter. Not that Ma was mad with me, she was just too distraught about Ryder to notice things like shoes. I felt so guilty … maybe if I had run faster, if Ryder hadn't tried to stick with me. I still ask myself, what if that takkie hadn't come off? Would Ryder have been arrested? Would he have died?'

Adeela withdraws her hand from Victor's and pulls at her cardigan. 'Someone found me and took me home. It was dark already. Ma put me in her bed and gave me something bitter to make me sleep. I was only seven, turning eight. They never told us how he died.'

Victor stands at the French windows with his back to her. The wind has picked up a little. The tree's branches scratch lightly against the glass. What, apart from platitudes, is there to say? What words …?

'I think,' she says, 'I should lie down a little now. We were up very early this morning, Lilly and me.' Adeela grips the arms of the chair and tries to lever herself out of it. She feels exhausted and the pain is making her nauseous. 'I'm sorry, Victor, to rattle on so. I don't know what's got into me this morning.'

Victor helps her to her feet.

'You will come again tomorrow, won't you?' she says. 'You and Vanezu? I want you to meet Sukey.'

Together they cross the faded Persian, and into her room. Next to the three-quarter bed, with its thick down duvet, though it is only fall, is a table with her medicine, a stainless-steel dish, a glass of water, and an old-fashioned travel alarm clock that folds into its own ruby-coloured leatherette case. Her customary pile of books has been replaced by the nurse's green plastic file. Even Adeela's reading glasses are gone. The bedding is already turned down, and the curtain half-drawn. Victor helps her lie down, kisses her gently on the forehead.

'We were good together, weren't we.' She says it as a statement.

II. Lilly

It is eleven o'clock when Lilly comes through the front door. She has been gone just a little more than an hour but is already anxious about her mother.

Victor takes the groceries from her and starts to pack them away in the small kitchen: skim milk; eggs; a small piece of fresh fish; miso soup; half a watermelon, the seeds dark and slick; a bunch of roses; coffee and bagels.

Lilly walks across the sitting room, noticing as she passes that her mother's cup of tea is still three-quarters full. A white film has settled on the surface. Adeela's room, it used to be Lilly's, is no more than an alcove off the living room, but it has a huge sash window filling up the external wall and it looks out onto the tree. She thinks of it as her mother's tree, though it really belongs, she supposes, if it belongs to anyone at all, to old Mr Cohen on the ground floor. Grumpy old fart.

They swapped rooms the day Lilly turned seventeen. It was her mother's idea; she wanted to simplify – at least that's what Lilly remembers her saying.

Lilly is up the ladder, painting the walls of her new room Plascon's sun-kissed yellow when the intercom buzzes, so Adeela puts down her roller and peels the latex gloves from her hands. They're just about done anyway. The intercom buzzes again. And again.

'Hurry up, Mom,' Lilly says.

Adeela presses the button for the speaker. 'Who is it?' she asks.

'Hi, Mrs K. It's us. Is the birthday girl in?'

'Vanezu?'

'And Donna and Loren. We've got cake.'

Adeela buzzes them in, but it is Lilly who flings the front door open and goes out into the hall. She can hear voices coming up the stairwell, the sound of feet. Somebody is wearing heels, probably Donna. Lilly half-expects Mr Cohen to yell at them for making such a racket. Then a moment later there they are filling the landing, her very best friends. Donna is carrying a chocolate-raspberry cake from Mila's Cake Shoppe. Loren has a bunch of yellow lilies.

'My favourites!' Lilly squeals.

Adeela rescues the cake and flowers while the girls fling their arms around each other, shepherds them into the apartment.

'For you.' Vanezu produces a bottle of Californian sparkling wine from the bottom of her tote bag and offers it to Adeela with a kiss. 'From my dad, for putting up with Lilly for seventeen years.'

The candles are lit. They sing 'Happy Birthday'. Lilly stands leaning over the table, her long black hair hangs straight and smooth as an ironed sheet on either side of her face. She clasps it out of the way with one paint-freckled hand, and blows the candles out.

'Make a wish,' Adeela says.

Under Lilly's white vest, apple-pert breasts fill the lace-edged bra with such confidence that a spasm of longing for her once-little girl catches in Adeela's throat. It is all right, she tells herself. This is how it goes. These are her friends. I am her family. They will lie on the couch, they will drink my champagne, they will eat one modest slice of cake each (except for Loren who will sneak another when she clears the plates), they will listen to music and talk about boys. They will check their mobiles constantly and respond to messages while continuing their conversation. They will see what others are up to, then plan where to go. They will discuss what to wear. These are the things girls this age do. And on Monday, they will go to school, and not prison. This is, after all, how a girl should be spending her seventeenth birthday. This is 2011, New York.

Lilly passes her a piece of cake and a glass of champagne. 'Are you still going to get that poetry book today?' she asks.

Her mother takes the hint. 'See you girls later,' Adeela says. 'I'll be back in time to make you some supper before you go out. How about pasta with roasted baby tomatoes and parmigiana (Lilly's current favourite), and a nice big green salad?' She waves from the door.

Lilly knows that after clearing away the supper things, her mother will sit in her favourite chair and read the poems in her new book one by one. She knows this because her mother insists that's the only way to read poetry, slowly, expectantly, the way you eat oysters. The magic, she always says, comes after you swallow. Lilly knows her mother will go to bed in the little alcove room with the curtains not yet hung before she gets home. What she doesn't know is that during the early hours of the morning Adeela will confuse the light left on in the window opposite with the bulb in the interrogation room, and wake up frightened.

Lilly has forgotten what the doctor said to her. The exact words probably don't matter that much. She remembers more clearly the spread of colour up the doctor's face, the way the tiny veins webbed across her cheeks seemed to light up, how her eyes narrowed. She must have taken the time to put make-up on that morning – there was a smudge of blue mascara just above her right eye. She must have drawn her hand across her face before coming into the room to speak to Lilly. The treatment wasn't having any effect any more. There wasn't anything else left to try. Not a whole lot to say, really.

Lilly calls Victor; he'll come over at once. Then she skypes Sukey.

'Oh, Lilly,' Sukey says, her short curly hair all tousled from sleep, her mouth moving slower than her voice. 'I'll get an earlier flight. I'll be there as soon as I can.'

This is the plan. It has all been discussed. Lilly knows what she is expected to do. She and her mother and Victor have worked it all out. She knows they are to engage Crystal from Central Hospice to help. She knows Victor is executor of her mother's will. There is enough money for college and she is already the legal owner of their apartment.

It's almost noon. Lilly says goodbye to Victor. He holds her face in his hands and kisses the top of her head.

'She was pretty talkative this morning,' he says. 'Probably wore her out. That and all the excitement about Sukey coming.' But they both know she is more than just tired.

Lilly goes to pick up the tea mugs near her mother's chair. There's a box with its lid lying to one side. Lilly stops. She recognises it immediately for what it is. She has helped her mother prepare for the memory box workshops she used to run as a counsellor at the HIV/Aids centre.

Lilly knows that on the lid there will be a self-portrait of her mother. She knows that her name and her birthday will be written underneath it. She knows, without looking, that there will be a space left open where Lilly can write in the date Adeela dies. She knows it will be soon.

Lilly kneels on the floor next to the coffee table. She cannot read the writing on the side of the box, though she knows it will be a timeline charting the events of her mother's life. She cannot read the writing because of the tears in her eyes.

'Lilly,' says Adeela. She is standing in the doorway, leaning against the wide, white-painted Oregon pine frame. 'Lilly. Lilly. Lilly.' She crosses the room and lowers herself onto the floor, holds onto her daughter. They cling to each other, but it is Lilly who is propping Adeela up.

Lilly helps Adeela into her chair, fetches a glass of water, then sits on the stool Victor sat on only hours before. The kitchen clock, a replica (though granted, it's somewhat smaller) of the one in Grand Central Station, says twelve forty-five. Crystal is only due at two to administer today's pain meds.

'Shall I call Crystal, ask her to come earlier?'

'Uh,' says Adeela, 'I'll be okay for a while still.'

Lilly lays her head on the armrest of her mother's chair. Its familiar, slightly dusty smell is mingled with something sharper, something menacing. She wants to burrow her head into her mother's side like she did when she was little. Wants her mother to smell the way she smells when they've been lazing in the sun. Or out in the wind. Wants her to smell of pancakes, or of the spicy lamb casseroles she calls bredie, of the chopped dhanya Americans call cilantro. Not this sharp, impersonal smell that tastes metallic in her mouth.

Adeela strokes her head. Lilly's hair has been cut into a Chinese bob and Adeela tucks a stray end behind her daughter's ear. At the base of her neck, just where it begins to curve into her shoulder, is a small tattoo, the shape of the African continent.

'I was sure you were a girl, long before they could tell one way or the other, and by then I was already calling you Lilly,' Adeela says. 'When I went into labour, I knew I had chosen the right name. I knew you would arrive that night, even though you were taking so long. And you did. Quarter past eleven on the 25th of September. The same day as Lillian Ngoyi.'

'Who?' Lilly lifts her head and looks at her mother. 'Was she an aunt or something?'

Adeela is quiet, looking out the open French window, at her tree.

'Somebody in South Africa, or somebody here?' Lilly prompts. Her mother hardly ever talks about her family, doesn't like to talk about living in South Africa much at all.

'They called her the Mother of Black Resistance, the woman I named you after.' Adeela takes a sip of water. 'Have a look in the box, Lilly. There are a few pictures of her, near the top.'

Lilly puts the box onto her lap and lifts out a clutch of papers. There is a set of black-and-white commemorative postcards tied in a striped ribbon. She pulls the ribbon, takes a card and turns it over to look at the photo. A middle-aged African woman looks away from her, her eyes gazing off to one side from beneath a high, pointed forehead framed by tightly combed-back hair. There are deep lines running down from the sides of her nostrils to the edges of her wide-mouthed smile. It's a formal picture, taken in a studio, maybe.

'She looks like she's seen something that has made her really sad,' Lilly says, passing it to her mother. She always thought being named after a flower was lame, but she's not so sure about being named for some politico either.

Lilly looks at another postcard. Four women in old-fashioned clothes are linked arm in arm; behind them is a crowd of women. One of the four is wearing a sari, another is in a smart suit with a handbag draped over her left arm. She has dark glasses on under a careful hairdo.

'That's Lillian.' Adeela points out the third woman, the one with a wide-collared shirt tucked into a full, calf-length skirt, two lines of braid stitched just above the hem. 'That's Helen Joseph' – she points to the dark glasses lady – 'and this is Albertinia Sisulu. I can't remember who this is just now. Her name will come to me ... Sophia something.'

'What are they doing? Looks like a march of some sort.'

'Yes,' says Adeela, 'a very famous women's march, in protest against the passbooks African people had to carry with them wherever they went.'

'So I am named Lilly after a South African activist? Not the flower?'

'Mhhh. I wanted to be like Lillian Ngoyi when I was a teenager. She was an incredible woman, Lilly.'

'What happened to her?'

'A few months after this picture was taken, she was arrested for high treason with hundreds of others, including Nelson Mandela. That was 1956, before I was born. She was kept locked up until she died. 1980. I started high school that year.

She wasn't just an activist, like those bourgeois types marching around Central Park shouting the odds for gay rights or gorillas in Uganda; she was a real heroine. She sacrificed her life fighting for an end to racism and sexism. I used to think our generation would finish that fight.'

Her mother is sitting upright in her chair now, twisting the big silver ring around and around her finger, staring straight ahead. Crystal said she would have energy surges. Is this what she meant? She looks kind of crazy. Lilly wishes Crystal would come. Her mother is sweating. Little beads of it line her top lip; there are damp stains under her arms – and she smells.

Lilly gets up to close the doors, pulls the curtain over a little, sits down again. What's with her mother, anyway? Why couldn't she just have left that damn box well alone. Why does she have to give her the whole damn name-story thing now? What difference does it make why she's named Lilly? Yeesh, but an activist?

'So you want me to go to law school rather than art school, then?' she says.

Adeela sinks back into her chair, puts a hand on Lilly's arm, 'I didn't call you Lilly because I wanted you to be an activist. I did it to remember how strong a woman can be when she really believes in something. Do you understand?'

Adeela takes a tiny piece of watermelon from the plate Lilly put next to her and takes a bite. Lilly watches. Enough chewing, she wants to yell. Swallow, damn it, swallow.

Adeela swallows. 'It's late for watermelons, isn't it?' she says. 'It is watermelon, isn't it?'

'Nice, huh? I found it this morning, down at Gianni's. Have another piece. Look, I took all the pips out.' Lilly knows her mother thinks it's criminal to eat anything that's been flown in from the other side of the world.

The watermelon feels good in Adeela's mouth, cool, like drinking from a Cape mountain stream, but it tastes like coal.

How does she know what coal tastes like? She doesn't really. Okay then, it tastes like black, pitch black. She knows what that tastes like.

Adeela takes another little bite. She wants to see Sukey tonight. Sukey who, like the watermelon (Lilly can't fool her) is also flying in from the other side of the world. And she wants to see Lillian turn nineteen. On Monday.

'I wasn't named for anyone in particular,' she says. 'Adeela is the Arabic word for equal.'

'Equal? To what?'

My father named me that because, he said, I was an equal disappointment to my mother and my sisters. He'd wanted a son.'

'Yeesh Mom. Why did your mother let him call you that?'

'I was born the day they first began demolishing houses in District Six, where I grew up. My mother said she could hear the bulldozers from where she lay in the Peninsula Maternity Hospital. By the time she got back home, a dozen houses in her neighbourhood were gone. My parents were among those who refused to move. It was a long, long fight. Eventually they gave up.'

'What's that got to do with your name?'

'Muslims believe it's a child's right to be honoured with a good name. The barakah of the name is its lifelong blessing. My mother believed in equality. She said I'd come out fighting and that she hoped I'd keep on fighting, all my life, for things like justice and equality. I couldn't do it though, Lilly. I tried, but I couldn't.'

'Mom, it's all right. Don't cry. Mom.'

Adeela has her eyes screwed closed. Even so, tears run down her cheeks.

'It's okay, Mom. It's okay. Really, don't cry.'

Adeela opens her eyes. She wants to tell Lilly she'll be all right, just give her a minute, but her daughter is only a silhouette with a voice that seems to come from the other side of the room. Adeela feels a band of dampness spreading down her back. The smell clogs her nostrils; she is repulsed by the stench, short of breath. The pain in her gut tightens. The glare hurts her head. The room seems to be fracturing into thousands of moving coloured pixels.

'Mom? Mom, are you okay? I think you'd better lie down now. Mom?'

Lilly half-carries her mother to the bedroom. Shit, where is Crystal? 'Crystal will be here any minute to give you your meds, okay? Then you'll feel better and can have a good sleep,' she says. 'I promise I'll wake you in time for a bath before Sukey gets here. Okay, Mom? We can wash your hair and I'll get out the new sweatpants Vanezu brought you at the GAP sale and your favourite polo neck. Okay, Mom?' Lilly is close to tears. 'Okay?'

'I want to tell you ...' Adeela whispers.

'No more talking, Mom, okay? Sukey can tell me everything, all right, Mom? Here. I'm going to give you some oxygen.' Lilly unhooks the oxygen mask and fits it over Adeela's mouth and nose, slips the elastic behind her head, then lowers her gently onto the pillow. She turns the dial and checks the flow. Where the fuck is Crystal? Of all days to be late.

Lilly sits on the edge of her mother's bed, watches her chest as her breathing slowly eases. She takes her mother's hand and begins to hum 'Thula Baba'. It's a Zulu lullaby Adeela used to sing her when she was little. Hush now, be quiet.

But Adeela is restless; her free hand picks at the duvet cover. Her left leg jerks in a sudden spasm of pain. Lilly wonders if she should administer the morphine herself. Should she give her mother a sedative? Maybe wait five more minutes. She wishes Vanezu would come, or Victor.

Lilly closes her eyes and sings louder. She sings all the names she can remember her mother ever mentioning: Ryder, Huda, Amina (not that she's ever met or even spoken to any of them) and Russell, her own father, killed, Sukey tells her much later, before she was born. She sings the places Adeela has mentioned on those rare occasions she talked about 'home' at all: District Six, Table Mountain, Lavender Hill (where drug lords and gangsters rule and little kids are killed in the crossfire – she's read about it in the *New York Times*).

'Thula thu, thula South Africa, thula wena.' She sings for Vanezu and for Victor, their longing for Zimbabwe. She sings for Adeela's homesickness. 'Thula thu, thula mama, thula thu.' And for her own ache to be African.

III. Crystal

Crystal has a key, but always uses the buzzer, just to let them know she's arrived and on her way up. She doesn't like surprising her patients. She pauses on the landing to catch her breath, unlocks the front door and steps into the apartment. Things are not going well. She knows that before she has taken three steps. Lilly is in Adeela's room, crooning. The French windows are wide open and the curtains are standing straight out in the stiff breeze. As if it wasn't chilly enough anyhow.

Crystal crosses the room and closes the doors, startling a little bird, one of those nondescript sorts she doesn't know the name of, from its perch. She turns her back on the tree and looks around. The room is tidy, really very tidy, except for an old painted cardboard box (one of Lilly's latest creations? Hell no! She knows what that is) and a few leaves blown across the floor. The magazines and newspapers have been tidied away. The poetry book she gave Adeela last Thanksgiving is lying on the kitchen table. Crystal recognises the cover at a glance: a naked woman with two pendulous breasts half shielded behind a hand whose fingers are thickened by age or disease. *Body Bereft*, that's the title. The poet's a South African. She thought Adeela might like that, regardless of whether the poems were shit or not. Crystal couldn't tell. She didn't know a shitty poem from a good one, not back then. Next to the book is a bunch of white roses, the tips tinged dark green just where the petals begin to curve slightly away from each other. They are still in their plastic sleeve. The place looks poised for a party.

Ah, yes. This is the day Adeela's long-lost friend is coming from South Africa, Sue something. Crystal makes a mental note to put the roses in water as soon as she has a moment.

September 23, 15h00
Pulse rate high. Temperature 102.1 F. Breathing shallow.
Swallowing difficult. Patient required oxygen to stabilise.
Severe pain in lower back and abdomen. Circulation poor.
Urine: smoky. No bowel action.
Fluid intake: +/- 75 ml
Solid foods: 1 small piece of watermelon

Crystal flips back to the previous entries ... that's less than yesterday, less than the day before too. Actually it's the least she's eaten in a week. She will have to let Dr Wilson know.

Medication administered
80mg OxyContin

And she will have to speak to Lilly. Though the poor girl can probably tell.

Crystal can hear Lilly in the bathroom. Toilet flushing, the rush of water as she turns on the shower, groans from the old plumbing. She sits a moment, her back to her friend, and stares out the big sash window, past the tree with its wizened leaves to the slice of wall with half a window opposite. She wonders who lives there and what they are doing. She hopes they are thirty-something, having wild Saturday-afternoon sex, or cooking a meal together. That there are bright mango-coloured tulips in a vase, music playing ... jazz maybe, or something more upbeat.

Crystal wants to be invited over for dinner. She wants to go into the home of the healthy, the virile, the rosy-cheeked. She wants to suck marrow from big meaty bones, lick her fingers before wiping them on linen napkins. She wants to pick the olives out of a bowl of glossy green leaves. She wants to be offered a third helping of crushed potatoes with lashings of butter and cracked black pepper just so she can laugh and shake her head – No, I couldn't possibly manage another mouthful, thank you. She imagines licking a smear of chocolate mousse from the side of her lover's mouth. Yes, she imagines having a lover. Brazilian. Or French.

But Crystal is fifty-seven years old and newly divorced. She is shapeless the way rising dough is shapeless. Her hair is beautiful, though, long and thick. Crystal never colours it, is proud of how dark it still is. She keeps her hair coiled up in a twist at the back of her head and secures it with a large hair grip. This she does often during the day, letting it down and coiling it back up. Fastening it with the hair grip. She wears men's shirts, good quality and well cut, buttoned to her throat. Sometimes she adds a silk scarf or a long rope of heavy beads, sometimes an antique brooch. She is particular about wearing natural fibres close to her skin. She has two pairs of Levi jeans which she wears on alternate days. She likes the old 501s because she doesn't have to wrestle them over her hips.

Crystal sighs. She knows having a lover is as likely as Adeela seeing snow fall again.

They met, Crystal and Adeela, only three years ago, on the stairs outside the centre. Adeela had been standing face turned up to the falling snow. They were going to the same case meeting, had coffee together afterwards across the road where Crystal had noticed Adeela often before. She was always alone, always reading. Crystal did not read much. And certainly not poetry. Adeela had been gentle with her.

Later, they had cried and laughed over the poems in that book with the pendulous breasts. They had cried for the ranting poet who refused to keep silent about being a woman caught between ageing and death. They had sobbed for Adeela, who had a one-in-a-hundred chance of seeing old age. They had cried for the soon-to-be-orphaned Lilly, sleeping in her room. And in among those tears, Crystal sobbed for herself.

Of all the poems they had read out loud to each other that night after Adeela came home from her double mastectomy, she remembers only two lines off by heart:

> *... this she knows: nobody will ever again breathlessly*
> *peel desire from her shoulders.*

Adeela is fast asleep. Crystal gets up and walks across to the kitchen table, picks up the book. She leafs through the pages, watching the familiar titles flip past till she reaches the inside front cover. She reads the note that she wrote:

> *Never give up!*
> *Thanksgiving – 22 November 2012*

Below it, a new inscription, in Adeela's handwriting, reads:

> *For Crystal*
> *May you live long enough for the tight to become loose,*
> *and may you revel in all those who are breathless in your*
> *company.*
> *A.*
> *22 September 2013.*

Crystal guiltily lays the book back on the table, feels she is trespassing. Tears claw up her throat, scald her sockets. She hears Lilly turn off the shower. She cannot cry now. Really, she should have known better than to nurse a friend. Crystal unwraps the cellophane from the flowers, picks out those already drooping and drops them into the stainless-steel trash-can. This is it. The very limit. She's going to quit, just as soon as Adeela goes. She can't do it any more.

Crystal fills a tall glass vase with water, adds the long-life mix and stirs, gathers up the roses and places them one by one into place, shifts them around a little. There. She lets out a little sigh of satisfaction.

What I'd really like to be, she thinks, is a florist.

Printed in the United States
By Bookmasters